"It's the holida...
family.

"The one that actually does want me around," Shane clarified. "I'm going to Los Angeles."

Gianna had a bad feeling about this. "For Christmas?"

He went on as if he hadn't heard her. "It's time for me to move on. Like you said, I found out what I came here for."

But was that all he'd found? What about her? What about the two of them? Instead she said, "What about the restaurant?"

"The sous chef can take over for me. I've trained her. No one is irreplaceable."

He was wrong about that. He couldn't be replaced in her heart. And that's when she knew she'd fallen in love with him.

Dear Reader,

In childhood we pick up the traditions that are carried on throughout our lives and one of the most time-honored is to spend the holidays with family. Everything's supposed to be perfect during this special season, at least that's what I thought as a little girl. One year, reality set in when my younger brother was in the hospital with pneumonia. He was a pretty sick kid. But on the morning of December 25, he was discharged and the whole family went to spring him. All of us were together which made the day even more special because it nearly didn't happen that way.

At Christmas most people make family plans, and Shane Roarke, the hero in this book, is no exception. But he takes it to the next level. Adopted as an infant, he's wondered all his life about the biological parents who gave him up. What he discovers about them will either give him more family than he's ever dreamed of or threaten his career and a future with Gianna Garrison, the woman he loves.

Life has taught me that things aren't always perfect. I make a conscious effort to treasure the crisis-free times and count on family for support during all the rest. But in my books there's always a happy ending and every day I'm grateful for this dream job.

I wish everyone health, happiness, love and peace at Christmas and all the best in the new year.

Happy holidays!

Teresa Southwick

THE MAVERICK'S CHRISTMAS HOMECOMING

TERESA SOUTHWICK

HARLEQUIN®
entertain, enrich, inspire™

Special thanks and acknowledgment to Teresa Southwick
for her contribution to the
Montana Mavericks: Back in the Saddle continuity.

Recycling programs
for this product may
not exist in your area.

ISBN-13: 978-0-373-65712-4

THE MAVERICK'S CHRISTMAS HOMECOMING

Copyright © 2012 by Harlequin books S.A.

www.Harlequin.com

Printed in U.S.A.

TERESA SOUTHWICK

lives with her husband in Las Vegas, the city that reinvents itself every day. An avid fan of romance novels, she is delighted to be living out her dream of writing for Harlequin.

To my brothers—Jim, Mike, Dan and Chris Boyle.
I love you guys. Merry Christmas!

Chapter One

When he'd come to Thunder Canyon five months ago look-ing for his biological parents, Shane Roarke never expected to find out that his father was in jail for stealing from the town. So far his mother's identity was still a mystery, but maybe that was for the best. Did he really want to meet the woman who'd shown the bad judgment to hook up with a criminal? And what did that say about his own DNA?

He'd arrived a city-slicker chef with a list of questions about who he was. Now he had half the answers and a lot to lose if anyone else found out. The information and what to do about it weighed heavy on his mind.

In June he'd taken the executive chef position at The Gallatin Room, the fine-dining restaurant at Thunder Can-yon Resort. With successful restaurants in L.A., New York and Seattle it had been a career step-down, but necessary for personal reasons. Now he was the definition of a man in conflict—part of him wished he'd never come, while the other part really liked this town.

"Oh, you're still here—"

Shane looked up from the glass of wine in front of him to the redhead who'd just walked into his kitchen. Gianna Garrison was a waitress and part-time bartender on his staff. In the big cities where he'd worked his name had been linked to models, actresses and celebrities, but he'd never seen a more beautiful woman than the one in front of him now, looking like a deer caught in headlights.

"I'm still here," he agreed.

"Like the captain of a ship."

"The last to leave." He smiled.

Gianna was wearing the black slacks and long-sleeved white shirt all the waitresses wore but it looked better on her. The tucked-in blouse accentuated breasts, not too big or too small, which only left just right. Her waist was trim, her legs slim and that curly, shoulder-length red hair always got his attention even from across a crowded room. Close-up was even better.

"Sorry to bother you." She started to back out of the room. "I'll just be going."

She wasn't bothering him. In fact she'd done him a favor. Shane realized the last thing he wanted was to be alone with his dark thoughts.

"Wait. We were a waitress short tonight." Pretty lame stating the obvious, but he'd just switched mental gears and it was the best he could come up with to stop her from leaving.

"Yeah, Bonnie has a bad cold. Coughing, sneezing and breathing germs on that party of ski executives from Switzerland seemed counterproductive to the goal."

Shane nodded. "Convincing them that Thunder Canyon

has the snow, slopes and service to make it a winter vacation destination for Europeans."

"Right. And have you seen any of those movies on the flu pandemic and how disease spreads? We wouldn't want Thunder Canyon identified as ground zero by the Centers for Disease Control. The Swiss would probably hear about it."

"That wouldn't be good. Bonnie was wise to call herself off."

The humor sparkling in her eyes made them almost turquoise. He hadn't noticed that before, which wasn't surprising. Between work, looking for his birth parents and feeling guilty about it on account of his real parents who loved him unconditionally, he'd been a little preoccupied. Now she was only a couple of feet away and he noticed that her eyes were wide and beautiful, like the Caribbean Ocean. If he wasn't careful, he could drown in them.

"So one waitress less means you worked twice as hard," he said.

She lifted one shoulder in a no-big-deal gesture. "I just moved faster, smiled more and dazzled them with the Garrison wit, hoping they had no idea it was taking just a little longer to get their orders delivered. The complimentary bottle of wine you sent over to the table didn't hurt, either. By the way, they raved about the food and seemed surprised. You'd think the invention of Swiss cheese entitled them to culinary domination of the universe."

"I'm guessing you didn't say that to them."

"No." She grinned.

"The head of the delegation complimented me on the food and service before they left. He promised me maximum stars, diamonds, happy faces, thumbs-up, however they designate their rating. Without you I couldn't have pulled that off, Gianna."

Her wit wasn't the only thing about her that dazzled. When she smiled, her face lit up like the town square decorated for Christmas. "I'm flattered you noticed."

"I make it my business to notice. It crossed my mind to come out to help serve, but I couldn't get away."

"Cooking is what you do. Delivering what you cook is my job."

"There's more to it than that. Even when the food is good it's not always easy to keep the customer happy. But you make it look easy. Tonight you did a fantastic job."

"I just handled it," she said modestly.

"You always do. You're one of my best waitresses. Thanks for all your hard work. I appreciate it very much."

"No problem. It's what you pay me for but it's nice to hear you say it." Gianna backed up a little more. "I'll just be going now."

No, he thought. Her dazzle kept the dark away and he wasn't ready for it to come back yet. He wanted her to stay. Saying that straight out might make her nervous, think he was hitting on her. That wasn't his intention. The pleasure of her company was his only goal; the question was how to achieve it.

All Shane could come up with was a delaying tactic. "Did you want something?"

"Why do you ask?"

"You came in the kitchen."

"Oh, that. It's just, you know—" Her shrug did interesting things to her breasts. "Tonight's special looked and smelled amazing so…"

"You're hungry." Of course. What other reason would she have for coming here when her shift was over. After a mental forehead slap, he said, "Doing the work of two people didn't leave time for a dinner break."

"It's my own fault. I missed the staff meal before service started. I'll just grab something on the way home."

"No." He stood and walked over to her. "The least I can do is feed you. And there will be a glass of wine involved."

"Don't make a mess on my account. The dishwasher and prep crew already cleaned up."

"But I'm the boss. I have a nice Pino Grigio already uncorked and it pairs well with the spinach and crab ravioli." He led her to the stool he'd just vacated then pressed gently on her shoulders, urging her to sit. The slight touch ignited a need in his belly and the instinct to pull her against him was unexpectedly powerful.

It was his business to notice workflow in the restaurant and he had. Just because it wasn't his job to be attracted to someone working the flow didn't make the attraction any less real. But he still wasn't hitting on her. This was just a gesture. A happy staff didn't quit and contented workers kept things running smoothly. Training a new waitress was time consuming and costly.

"I was going to have something myself. Please join me."

"Okay, then. Thanks." She rested her heel on the metal rung of the stool and crossed one leg over the other.

The movement was graceful, sexy, and it was an effort to pull his gaze away. On his first day at The Gallatin Room, Gianna Garrison had caught his eye, but for professional and personal reasons he'd resisted the impulse to act on the temptation. Until tonight.

Just before Thanksgiving he'd received conclusive proof that Arthur Swinton, the most hated man in Thunder Canyon, was his biological father. The information had weighed on him over the last couple of days and he was low on willpower. That was the best explanation he could come up with for this lapse in professional judgment. It was time to do his chef thing and take his mind off other things.

While he worked assembling plates, warming food, pouring wine, Gianna chattered away. He let her, liking the sound of her voice, the warm honey with just a hint of gravel. Then something she said tapped into his dark mood again.

"The Thanksgiving dinner you prepared last week for military families was amazing. Everyone in town is talking about it. Angie Anderson and Forrest Traub told me how thrilled the families were, how special and appreciated they felt for their loved ones' sacrifices."

He'd been more preoccupied than usual since that night. People had looked at him like he walked on water and he felt like a fraud. How could he be a walk on water type when Arthur Swinton was his biological father? The man had been convicted and sent to jail for embezzling public funds. Not only that, he'd perpetrated a conspiracy to ruin the Traubs, one of the most prominent families in town. If there was someone who didn't hate Swinton, Shane hadn't met them yet.

Gianna smiled at him. "They said it really helped because of missing their loved ones overseas so much, especially around the holidays."

"I know something about missing family," Shane whispered.

"What's that?" she asked.

He slid hot food onto two plates, then looked over his shoulder. "You're missing something if you don't eat this while it's hot."

"It looks wonderful and smells even better."

He put the two steaming plates on the stainless-steel countertop, then pulled up another stool and sat at a right angle to her. "Dig in."

"Okay." After she did, her gaze met his. "This is sinfully good. I don't even want to think about the calories."

"It's a little-known fact that when you do the work of two people calories don't count."

"Thank goodness. Because this tastes even better than it smells and it smells very fattening." She licked a drop of white wine sauce from her lower lip.

For a second, Shane thought he was going to choke on his own food. The look on her face was the most unconsciously erotic thing he'd ever seen.

A sip of wine kick-started his brain again and he managed to say, "I'm glad you like it."

The words almost made him wince. He had a reputation for being charming but tonight he wouldn't win any awards for witty repartee. It was a miracle that she didn't make an excuse and run for the hills.

"How do you like Thunder Canyon?" She took another bite and chewed.

"Actually, I love it."

"Seriously?" She stared at him as if he had two heads.

"Cross my heart. If it's not at the top of my list, it's very close."

"But you've been all over the world, no?"

"Yes."

"Where did you go to culinary school?"

"CIA."

"Does that mean you could tell me but you'd have to kill me?" The corners of her full mouth turned up.

"The Culinary Institute of America. Hyde Park, New York. About two hours from Manhattan."

"Convenient."

He nodded. "I got a degree in Culinary Arts management because I always wanted to open my own restaurant. But I went to Paris to learn baking and pastry arts. I've traveled to Italy and Greece to experience various cooking techniques like liquid nitrogen chilling, and experience different cuisines. CIA also has a campus in Napa where they specialize in a different area of food preparation and wine pairing."

"So you've got a well-rounded culinary education."

"Yes. My parents are well-to-do. I didn't have to worry about student loans and could indulge every aspect of my curiosity about business trends and cutting-edge themes in the food-service industry."

Her eyes filled with a little wonder and a lot of envy. "That sounds so exciting. How can the town square in Thunder Canyon, Montana, compare to the Eiffel Tower? The Louvre? The—everything—of France?"

"Paris is something to see. No question. But it's not fair to compare places in the world. The favorites just speak to your heart."

"And Thunder Canyon speaks to yours?"

"Yes." It was true, but she probably thought he was a poetic idiot.

He didn't understand his instant connection to this small town in Montana so far off the beaten path. It crossed his mind that the answer could be in his DNA, but that didn't make sense. Not really. Arthur Swinton was a greedy opportunist who only cared about himself and that had nothing to do with the place that filled up his son's soul.

"I'd like to hear about you," he said. "Are you from here?"

"Born and raised. My mother, father, sister and her family are still here." She put the fork down on her empty plate. "After getting a business degree, I went to New York."

"And?" He poured a little more wine in her glass. "What did you do there?"

"I opened a travel agency."

"So, you took a bite out of the Big Apple." Brave girl. He was impressed. His first business venture had been close to home in L.A. She jumped right into the big time. "Apparently I'm not the only one who's been all over the world."

She lifted her shoulder, a noncommittal gesture. "I was pretty busy getting the company off the ground."

"It's a lot of work, but incredibly exciting turning a dream into reality."

"Speaking of reality," she said, clearly intending to change the subject. "You certainly turned your appearance on that reality cooking show—*If You Can't Stand the Heat*—into culinary success."

"I was lucky."

"Oh, please. If you call talent, charm, good looks and a clever way with a wooden spoon luck, then I'm the Duchess of Cambridge."

He laughed. "So you think I'm not hard on the eyes?"

"Are you kidding? You're gorgeous." She looked a little surprised that the words had come out of her mouth. "But, for the record, really? That was your takeaway from what I just said?"

It was better than wondering where his looks had come from. "Beauty is as beauty does."

"What does that even mean?"

"You got me. Do you have someone running the travel agency?" Which begged another question. "Why are you here in Thunder Canyon?"

"Personal reasons." The sparkle disappeared from her eyes and she frowned before quickly adding, "I'm only here for a little while. Not much longer."

Shane understood personal reasons and the reluctance to talk about them so he didn't ask further. "Are you anxious to get back?"

"Who wouldn't be?" She took the stem of her wineglass and turned it. "There's a rumor that your contract here at The Gallatin Room is only six months."

"Yeah." He'd thought that would give him enough time to find out what he wanted to know, but he'd only found out half of it. Now the question was whether or not to keep going and what to do with the information he already had. "So it seems both of us have a time limit here in town."

It was weird, probably part of the pathetic, poetic streak kicking in tonight, but talking to her had made him realize that since coming here he'd been a loner. And suddenly he was lonely. But the last thing he needed in his life was a long-term romantic complication. She was beautiful, funny and smart. He wanted to see her again and she wasn't staying in town. That made her the perfect woman.

"I guess you could say I have a time limit here," she agreed.

"Then we shouldn't waste any time. Have dinner with me."

She looked at his empty plate. "Didn't we just do that?"

"Sassy." He grinned and added that to her list of attributes. "I meant something away from work. Monday is the only day the restaurant is closed and every place within a twenty-mile radius is, too. How about I cook for you at my condo? It's not far, here on the resort grounds."

"I know. But—"

"It's just a home-cooked meal. How does six-thirty sound?"

"I don't know—" Her expression said she was struggling with an answer.

That's when he gave her the grin that reality show enthusiasts had called his secret ingredient. "Doing double-duty tonight deserves a double thank-you."

"When you put it that way… How can I say no?"

"Good. I look forward to it."

Gianna had been looking forward to this evening since Shane Roarke had invited her to dinner. She took the elevator to the third floor of the building on Thunder Canyon

Resort grounds where his condo was located. After five months of nursing a crush on him she could hardly believe he'd finally asked her out. Or in. It felt surreal, with a dash of guilt for good measure.

What she'd told him about herself in New York was a little sketchy. She hadn't so much taken a bite out of the Big Apple as been chewed up and spit out by it. Apartments were small and expensive. The travel agency didn't survive, a casualty of the internet, with more people looking online, eliminating the middle man. And the recession. And she'd seen no point in sharing with Shane that she kept falling into the trap of choosing men who had no intention of committing.

She hadn't lied about personal reasons bringing her back to Thunder Canyon. It was the elaborating part she'd left out. Being unemployed and penniless *were* personal and her primary motivation in coming home. A job at The Gallatin Room was getting her back on her feet. She had a small apartment above the new store Real Vintage Cowboy and the only car she could afford was a fifteen-year-old clunker that she hoped would hold together because she couldn't afford a new one. Sharing all of that with a sexy, sophisticated, successful man like Shane Roarke wasn't high on her list of things to do.

After stepping out of the elevator she walked down the thick, soft carpeted hall to the corner apartment, the one with the best views.

"Here goes nothing," she whispered, knocking on the door. Moments later Shane was there. "Hi."

"You're very punctual." He stepped back and pulled the door wider. "Come in. Let me take your things."

She slipped out of her long, black quilted coat and handed it to him along with her purse, then followed as he walked into the living room. It was stunning. The wood entryway opened to a plush beige carpet, white overstuffed sofa, glass tables and twelve-foot windows on two sides. High ceilings held recessed lighting and the expanse of warm, wheat-colored walls were covered with artwork that looked like it cost more than she made in a year.

"Wow." Gianna had been nervous before but now her nerves got a shot of adrenaline. "This is beautiful."

"I think so, too." Shane's gaze was firmly locked on her face.

Her heart stuttered and skidded. His eyes weren't the color of sapphires or tanzanite, more like blue diamonds, an unusual shade for a stone that could cut glass. Or turn icy. Right this second his gaze was all heat and intensity.

"I've never seen you in a dress before. Green is your color," he said. "It looks beautiful with your hair."

Outside snow blanketed the ground; it was December in Montana, after all. But this moment had been worth the cold blast of air up her skirt during the walk from her clunker of a car. She'd given tonight's outfit a lot of thought and decided he saw her in black pants most of the time. Tonight she wanted him to see her in something different, see her in a different way. The approval on his face as he glanced at her legs told her it was mission accomplished.

"'Tis the season for green."

She'd never seen him out of work clothes, either. The blue shirt with long sleeves rolled up suited his dark hair and brought out his eyes, she thought. Designer jeans fit his long legs and spectacular butt as if made especially for him. For all she knew they might have been.

"Would you like some chardonnay?"

"Only if it pairs well with what you're cooking," she answered.

"It does."

She followed him to the right and into the kitchen with

state-of-the-art, stainless-steel refrigerator, dishwasher and cooktop. It was most likely top-of-the-line, not that she was an expert or anything. Ambience she knew something about and his table was set for two with matching silverware, china and crystal. Flowers and candles, too. The ambience had date written all over it.

"Good to know. Because I'm sure the food police would have something to say about nonpaired wine."

"I kind of am the food police."

"That makes one of us." She took the glass of wine and sipped. Not too sweet, not too dry. It was delicious. The man knew his wine and from what she'd been able to dig up on him, he knew his women, too. She was really out of her depth. "And it's kind of a relief that you know your stuff. Because you know that thing about actors wanting to direct? I don't think it works the same in food service. Waitresses don't want to be chefs. At least I don't. Boiling water I can do. Ham sandwich, I'm your girl. Anything fancy? Call someone else. Call you. You're famous in food circles for—"

He stopped the babbling with a finger on her lips. "Call me for what now?"

"You tell me." She took a bigger sip of wine and nearly drained the glass.

"You're nervous." He was a master of understatement.

"I didn't think it showed."

"You'd be wrong." He smiled then pulled chicken, vegetables and other ingredients from the refrigerator—all obviously prepared in advance—and stuff from a cupboard beside the stove, probably seasoning or spices. Or both. He took out a well-used frying pan and placed it on the stove. "But I'm pretty sure I understand."

"What?"

"Your nerves. Thanks to reality TV, exposure about everything from bachelors to swamp people, we chefs have earned something of a reputation."

"What kind of reputation would that be?" She finished her wine, then set the glass on the granite countertop.

"Bad boy." The devil was in the blue-eyed glance he tossed over his shoulder. "And I'm no exception."

"Oh?"

"Think about it. What I do involves sharp knives and fire. Very primitive." As he lit the burner on the stove, the fire popped as the gas ignited.

"I see what you mean." And how.

"On top of that I invited you to my place for dinner. But let me assure you that I have no intention of making you the dessert course."

"That never crossed my mind." But why not? she wanted to ask. It hadn't been on her mind until just now. Well, maybe a little bit when she saw him in that shirt and those jeans because that kicked up a curiosity about what he'd look like *without* them.

He glanced over his shoulder again while tossing in the air over the hot flame everything he'd put in that frying pan. "In spite of what you may have heard, I'm not that type. I like to get to know a woman."

If he really got to know her, chances were pretty good that he'd lose interest. And speaking of types, she probably wasn't his. She wasn't a businesswoman now, more the still-trying-to-find-herself variety.

"So, what are you doing for Christmas?" Changing the subject had seemed like a great idea until those words came out of her mouth. Would he think she was hinting for an invitation? The filter between her brain and mouth was either pickled or fried. Or both.

"My holiday plans are actually still up in the air," he said. There was an edge to his voice that demanded another subject change so she did. "What are you making for dinner tonight?"

"It's something I'm experimenting with."

"So I'm the guinea pig?"

"Think of yourself as quality control." He grabbed the two plates off the table, then slid half the contents of the frying pan onto each one and set them on a part of the cooktop that looked like a warming area. Then he put liquids into the sauté pan and stirred, fully concentrating on the job. After spooning what looked to her like rice from a sauce pan, he said, "Dinner is served." He glanced at her. "More wine?"

"Please."

After filling her glass and setting plates on the table, he held the chair for her to sit down. If a guy had ever done that before, she couldn't remember. Then he sat across from her. The star lilies and baby's breath with candles in crystal holders on either side gave it all a romantic feel.

Suddenly her appetite disappeared, but she was here to eat and figured she'd better do that. She took a bite of the chicken and the flavors exploded on her tongue. "Oh, my. That is so good. It's like a party in my mouth and I thought only chocolate could do that."

"I'm glad you like it."

"What's in here?" She chewed and swallowed. "Can you tell me or would you have to kill me?" At his wicked look she shrugged. "Bad-boy rep, remember? CIA. Fire. Sharp stuff."

"I'll make an exception for you." He picked through the food on his plate. "Chicken. Asparagus. Mushrooms."

"This looks like rice, but the consistency is wrong."

"It's risotto."

"Ah." The gleam in his eyes started pressure in the vicinity of her chest and she hoped it was nothing more than pre-indigestion.

They ate in silence for several moments before he said, "So how was growing up in Thunder Canyon?"

"It was great, but keep in mind that I didn't know anything else." She put down her fork and wiped her mouth on the cloth napkin. "The pace is slower here and kids don't need to grow up so fast."

"It's slower for grown-ups, too."

Gianna nodded. "Not everyone is happy about that. Maintaining the balance between status quo and development has been and probably still is a source of conflict here in town."

That started a discussion about everything from population growth to weather to large holiday groups scheduled at The Gallatin Room the following week. It was interesting to hear about restaurant management, all that went into a successful business besides just preparing food. Time seemed to both fly and stand still.

Finally Shane looked at her. "Would you like more?"

"No, thanks." Her plate was empty and she was so full. "I guess guinea *pig* was the correct term."

"I don't think so. Clearly you enjoyed the food. In some cultures burping is high praise and a compliment to the chef."

"And in some parts of the country it's a competitive sport."

He laughed, then stood and picked up his plate. She followed his lead and carried hers into the kitchen, where he took it from her and set them in the sink.

"What can I do to help?" she asked.

"Nothing. You're a guest and I have a housekeeper. Why don't we sit in the living room?"

"Okay." But when they walked in, the tall windows were filled with the sight of lights winking in the valley below and she walked over. "That is a pretty amazing view."

"I think so. Would you like to see it from the balcony?"

"Oh, yes." She might never have another chance.

Shane opened the French door, then let her precede him outside. The cold air hit her immediately, but when they moved to the railing and he stood beside her, his nearness and the warmth from his body took the edge off.

"Oh, Shane, this is so stunning. Is it always like this?"

"Well, the mountains are permanent and don't change."

"Duh."

He grinned down at her, then pointed. "See the spotlights over there? That's the slopes and they're always illuminated for night skiing. But in the last few days since Thanksgiving, people are putting up Christmas decorations so everything is even more beautiful."

She glanced at him. "There's something in your voice, an awe, a respect, as if you're whispering in church."

"It kind of feels that way," he admitted. "There's a sense of being in the presence of God. The natural beauty here..."

"Speaks to your heart?"

"Yeah. I do love it. Especially on a night like this."

She looked up at the moon and stars. "I don't know what's more beautiful, the sky above or valley below."

"Maybe it isn't either one."

There was a raspy quality in his voice that made her look at him. Their gazes locked and his sparked with heat and intensity. His shoulders were wide, his arms strong. Suddenly she was filled with an ache to feel them around her. She *wanted* to be dessert.

As if Shane could read her thoughts, his mouth inched toward hers and again time stood still.

Until it didn't.

One second passed with him just standing there, then two before he backed away even though the expression in his eyes hadn't changed. "It's getting late. I should probably see you to your car."

Gianna blinked up at him wondering what just happened. She wasn't so out of practice that she didn't know when a man was going to kiss her, and Shane had been about to do that. Something had changed his mind, but darned if she knew what it was. But clearly she'd been dismissed for unknown reasons.

"It is getting late. I'll just get my coat."

Shane got her things, and if the atmosphere at the restaurant was as awkward as the walk down to where she'd parked her wreck of a car, work was going to be even less fun than being one waitress short while feeding the Swiss delegation.

Chapter Two

Three days later Gianna was stewing in The Gallatin Room kitchen, which was ironically appropriate. It had been three nights since Shane had made dinner for her at his place. Three nights of seeing him at the restaurant where they both worked and he hadn't said a word to her—not about work, not even about things other than work. Even a hello, how are you, wasn't in his repertoire. In fact he was going out of his way to ignore her and she didn't understand why.

She also didn't have time to think about it. Waitresses were hurrying in and out of the kitchen with orders and busboys handled trays of dirty dishes, utensils and glassware. It was busy and noisy and she was putting together a basket of bread for the order she'd just taken. Shane stood by the stove concentrating on sautéing seafood over a hot flame. She stared at his back and felt like a lovelorn idiot, but she couldn't help it. When he was in a room her gaze automatically searched him out.

He, on the other hand, didn't even look at her when he wasn't cooking. Disappointment trickled through her and she felt incredibly stupid. Maybe she'd been hoping the third time was the charm—or third day post dinner he would finally break his silence.

No such luck.

Bonnie Reid pushed through the swinging doors separating the kitchen areas from the dining room. Her friend did break the silence.

"Wow, it's busy in there tonight, G."

"Tell me about it."

Gianna rested her hip against the stainless-steel worktable. She'd become good friends with the other waitress, a petite brunette with a pixie haircut and big brown eyes. They'd both been hired at about the same time and bonded over the good, the bad and the awe of their celebrity boss. The other night she'd thought he actually was awesome, but now? Not so much.

"I'm very glad you're over your cold and back to work." Gianna dragged her gaze away from Shane and looked at her friend.

There was sympathy in those brown eyes. "If I hadn't been too sick to crawl out of bed, I'd have been here. It must have been awful by yourself, serving that big party of Swiss businessmen."

"I managed." And now she heard Shane's voice in her head, telling her she always did. The words still made her glow, but she was doing her best to get over it.

"I hated leaving you shorthanded. You must have run your legs off."

Gianna looked down. "Nope. Still there. Cellulite, the extra two and a half pounds on each thigh and all."

"Yeah. Right." Bonnie grinned. "You're fit and fine, my friend."

"Not that anyone would notice." She glanced at Shane who still had his back to her.

"Did something happen while I was out sick?" Bonnie's tone was sharp with curiosity, but fortunately their boss was too far away to hear in the noisy kitchen. "What did I miss?"

"Nothing." That was the very sad truth, Gianna thought.

"I'm getting a vibe, G." Her friend glanced at Shane, then back. "Did Roarke the magnificent do something? Say something?"

"Said something, did absolutely nothing." Darn him. Gianna picked up the silver basket in which she'd artfully arranged a variety of herb-covered rolls and cheese cracker bread, then started to walk back to the dining room.

"Uh-uh. Not so fast." Bonnie shook her head. "You can't drop a cryptic comment like that and not elaborate. It violates every rule of friendship and is just wrong on so many levels."

"Really, nothing happened. I guess I just got the signals wrong. Wouldn't be the first time."

"You're trying to deflect me. Even if this is about all the time you wasted on too many men who have an allergy to commitment, it's not going to work. Did Roarke make a move on you?" Bonnie's eyes filled with indignant anger and she looked a little dangerous.

"Nothing like that." Gianna pulled her farther around the corner to make sure they couldn't be overheard even with the sizzle of cooking and banging of utensils. "We had a moment."

"What kind of moment?"

"When you called in sick I missed the staff dinner then did double duty and was starved at the end of my shift. I thought everyone had left and came in here to grab something to eat. Shane wasn't gone."

"You were alone with him? Did he try something?"

If only... "No. He made me food and gave me wine."

"To lower your resistance? I'll take him apart—"

"Stand down." Gianna couldn't help smiling at the thought of her tiny friend taking on tall, muscular, masculine Shane Roarke. "He asked me to dinner on Monday, at his place."

"How was it? His place, I mean. I've got more questions, but first things first."

"All I can say is rich people really are different."

"That good, huh?"

"The artwork. Furniture. Spacious floor plan and high ceilings. The lighting." She sighed at the memory. "And don't even get me started on the view."

"So he caught you in his web, or lair, or whatever, then pounced?" The fierce look was back.

"That's just it. He took me out on the balcony to show me the view of the mountains, the valley getting ready for Christmas. There was a moon and stars and lights stretching across said valley."

"Romantic with a capital *R*."

"Romantic with every letter capitalized and the whole word italicized." She sighed. "I was sure he was leaning in for a kiss and then—"

"What?"

"Nothing. He all but told me to go home, except he did it in his Roarke-like way. 'I'll see you to your car,'" she quoted.

"Bastard." Bonnie shook her head. "Gentleman bastard."

"I know." Gianna peeked at him again, busily sautéing something. "That was Monday night and he hasn't acknowledged me here at work since. I'm not sure which is worse. The let's-just-be-friends speech I'm used to or this cold shoulder."

Bonnie's frown went from fierce to puzzled. "I prefer the speech. At least you know where you stand."

Maybe that was her chronic problem, Gianna thought. If the relationship status wasn't spelled out, she went straight to hope. That meant she'd made no progress in breaking her bad habit of being a hopelessly romantic fool who wasted time on the wrong men.

"Anyway, that's the scoop." She angled her head toward the swinging doors. "I have to get back to work."

"Me, too." Bonnie gave her a sympathetic look. "I've got your back."

"Thanks."

Gianna put her shoulder to one of the kitchen's swinging doors, then opened it and walked into the quiet and elegant world where special service was the key to success. A beautiful setting during any season, The Gallatin Room was even more so, decorated for Christmas. A ten-foot tree with white lights, red, green and gold ornaments and shiny garland stood in the corner. All the tables had red poinsettias in the center on white linen tablecloths.

Now that Gianna had seen the view from Roarke's penthouse apartment, she knew this restaurant wasn't the most romantic place in Thunder Canyon, but she'd put it very high on the list. This was a weeknight but the place was nearly full, and that happened when you served the best food in town. That's what the two women at her table were after. Gianna had chatted them up while delivering menus and found out they were having a girls' long ski weekend.

She put the breadbasket on the table, then looked at the beautiful blonde and equally pretty brunette, both in their late twenties. "Have you decided or do you need another few minutes to look over the menu?"

"Too many tempting choices," the blonde said. "Do you know what you're having, Miranda?"

"I should go with salmon." She frowned, but her face didn't move. "But Shane's filet with that yummy sauce is to die for."

Gianna didn't recognize either woman and she had a good memory for faces. "So you've been here before?"

"Not here." Miranda shook her head. "But I've been to Roarke's in New York. Daisy and I do a winter ski trip every year and have been talking about trying the slopes in Thunder Canyon for a while. But we always decided on somewhere easier to get to that had restaurants with a reputation. Then we heard Shane Roarke was the chef here."

"He definitely is."

"Miranda says this menu is different from the one in New York," Daisy said.

"He's tailored his signature recipes specifically for The Gallatin Room. I can tell you that every one is fantastic."

"What's your favorite?" Daisy asked.

The chicken he'd made for her at his place. But that wasn't for public consumption yet. She smiled at the two women and hoped it was friendly because that's not the way she felt.

"It would be easier to tell you what's not my favorite. If you're in the mood for beef, the filet is excellent, practically melts in your mouth. And the sauce only enhances the flavor. I'm not a fan of lamb, but people who are rave about it here. The stuffed, grilled salmon is wonderful. And a little lighter, which would leave room for dessert."

"Tell me the chocolate, sky-high cake I had in New York is a choice."

"I don't know if it's the same, but there is one that will tempt you to lick crumbs off the plate."

"That does it." Miranda smiled in rapture. "Shane's desserts are the best. I'll have the salmon. Tell me about The Gallatin salad."

"It's greens with avocado, tomato and goat cheese in a very delicate dressing. So delicious you won't believe it's good for you."

"You talked me into it."

"Make it two," Daisy said. "And a bottle of the Napa Valley Chardonnay."

"Excellent choice." Gianna smiled at the two women. "On behalf of Thunder Canyon Resort and The Gallatin Room, I'll do everything possible to give you a perfect dining experience. If there's anything you'd like, just let me know. It's our goal to make this your ski vacation destination every year."

"Shane being the chef here made the difference in our choice this time," Miranda said.

"He's really something." Just what, Gianna wasn't sure.

"Is he by any chance here now?" Miranda asked.

"Every night."

"I'd love to say hello again." She looked at her friend. "And Daisy has never met him."

"I've certainly heard a lot about him," the blonde said. "Do you think he would come by the table?"

"I can ask." And that would give her an excuse to talk to him. "Although he's pretty busy."

"I understand. I'm not sure he'll remember me, but my name is Miranda Baldwin."

Gianna walked back to the kitchen and her heart was pounding at the thought of talking to Shane. Maybe it would break the ice. Give him a chance to say he'd just been too busy, up to his eyeballs in alligators what with Christmas parties and planning menu changes to shake things up with new dishes in January. It was a slim hope, but hope was something and a hard habit for her to break.

She went through the swinging doors into the kitchen and

saw Shane directing the sous-chef. He shifted to the cutting board on the stainless-steel table across from the stove.

"Can I talk to you?" she asked, moving beside him.

"What is it?" There was no anger or irritation in his tone. In fact there was no emotion at all, which was worse.

If only the world would open now and swallow her whole. Gianna felt her hope balloon deflate. His non-reaction made it unlikely that he would mention their dinner or anything about spending time with her. It was like nothing had ever happened. Situational amnesia. If he wasn't going to bring up the subject, neither would she.

"There's a Miranda Baldwin in the dining room who says she knows you from New York and wondered if she could say hello. I told her you might be too busy—"

"I can do that." He started toward the door and said over his shoulder, "Thanks."

"For nothing," she whispered under her breath.

In every serious relationship she'd had, the guy had strung her along and when it was time to fish or cut bait, she got cut. But Shane couldn't get away from her fast enough, which was a first. Apparently bad dating karma had followed her from New York and mutated.

Clearly he wasn't into her. Since she wasn't into wasting any more time, that should make her happy. Somehow it didn't.

Shane pushed through the double doors into the dining room and left Gianna behind in the kitchen with the hurt he'd caused evident in her eyes. She probably thought he was crazy and who could blame her? Certainly not him. He'd invited her to dinner, then stood with her looking at the night sky and wanting to kiss her more than he wanted his next breath. Every day since then he'd fought the urge to tug her into a secluded corner and see if her lips tasted as good as he imagined. There were times he wished he was as good with words as he was with food and this was one of those times.

He liked her, really liked her. The attraction was stronger than he'd felt in a very long time, maybe ever. He was still coming to terms with the truth about his father's identity so, for Gianna's sake, he wouldn't start something that he could really mess up. Cooling things was for the best and judging by the look on her face when he'd left the kitchen so abruptly, he'd done an exceptional job of it. The depth of emotion he'd seen proved that even though it would be temporary, she could get hurt and he wouldn't do that to her.

Looking over the bustling dining room a sense of satisfaction came over him. Revenue was up from this time a year ago and if that was because of him, he was glad. If the information about who his father was got out, that could keep him from drawing a local crowd, so he planned to enjoy this while it lasted.

Shane knew which tables Gianna had tonight and headed in that direction, then recognized Miranda. She was a beautiful brunette and asking her out had crossed his mind while he'd been in New York. Now she seemed ordinary compared to a certain redhead he wished he'd met while they'd both been there.

He stopped at the table. "Miranda, it's good to see you again."

"Shane." She smiled. "You remember me."

He didn't feel especially charming, but it was said that trait was what had won the reality cooking show and launched his career. He dug deep for it now.

"Of course I remember." He bent and kissed her cheek. "A woman like you is unforgettable."

"Then maybe it was my phone number you forgot. You never called me." Her eyes both teased and chastised.

"Believe me when I say that you're better off." It was easy to look sincere when telling the truth. "And there was no one else."

"Contrary to what the tabloids said."

"Because, of course, we all know that every word the rag sheets print is the honest truth." He grinned to take any sting out of that statement. "Truly, I had no personal life. It was all about opening Roarke's and keeping it open. I was practically working around the clock."

The blonde at the table cleared her throat, demanding her share of attention. "Hello, Mr. Roarke. I'm Daisy Tucker."

"It's a pleasure to meet you, Miss Tucker."

"Daisy. And the pleasure is all mine."

He didn't miss the flirty expression, the seductive tone, and there was a time when he'd have flirted back. Partly to fuel his reputation and get his name in the paper. Although he'd just mocked the tabloids, any marketing expert would tell you that even bad publicity is good, anything that gets your name out there. He was no expert, but knew the information that his biological father was a criminal would take bad publicity to a different, not good level.

"Shane," Miranda said, "after opening restaurants in so many big cities here in the States, I expected you to conquer London, Paris and Rome. It was really a surprise to find you were the executive chef here in off-the-beaten-path Montana."

"I had my reasons."

"But Thunder Canyon? What's the appeal?"

He spotted Gianna's bright hair across the room, just as she was coming out of the kitchen and a knot of need tightened in his belly. She wasn't the reason he'd taken the job but just being able to watch her was definitely appealing. The not-touching mandate was his cross to bear.

"That's difficult to put into words." He looked from one

beautiful face to the other. "I simply fell in love with Thunder Canyon."

"In that case," Miranda said, "maybe you could suggest some places to visit while we're here."

It was a hint for him to show them around and not a very subtle one. Even if he had the time, he wasn't interested. "It was actually love at first sight with Thunder Canyon. I haven't been here that long and haven't had time to explore much."

"Then maybe old friends from out of town is a good excuse to see the local highlights."

"As tempting as that would be, my schedule is really tight. I've got parties every weekend and several during the week until Christmas." It wouldn't be politically correct to tell her he wasn't interested. "You're better off checking with the concierge at your hotel."

"I'm very disappointed," she said.

"Me, too. You know what they say. This is the most wonderful time of the year."

"Ho, ho, ho." Miranda pretended to pout.

"It was wonderful to see you. Happy holidays." He kissed each woman on the cheek. "Duty calls."

He turned away and scanned the room, something he did frequently. It was a chance to make sure service was impeccable, that people were relaxed and happy. How he'd love to get a helping of happy for himself. Speaking of relaxed... He spotted a romantic booth for two and recognized the romantic couple occupying it.

Angie Anderson and Forrest Traub radiated love like a convection oven. That spontaneous thought begged the question: Where in the world had this recent poetic streak come from and when would he shake it?

He headed in their direction and when the two of them stopped gazing into each other's eyes for a moment, they spotted him. After weaving his way through the tables, he slid into the booth against the wall on the seat across from them. The other side had plenty of room for several more members of a platoon since Angie sat so close to Forrest, there was no space between them.

"Hi," he said to them.

"Merry Christmas." Angie was a college student and a volunteer at the town's teen hangout called ROOTS. In her early twenties, her shiny brown hair and dark eyes made her look like a teenager herself. "How are you, Shane?"

"Okay. What's up with you guys?"

"I'm counting the days until classes are over and it's vacation."

"Even with studying for finals she finds time to help the kids out with the holiday letters for soldiers." Forrest put his hand on hers, resting on his forearm. His hair was still military short and he had the muscular fitness and bearing of a soldier, even with the limp from a wound he'd sustained while deployed overseas.

"It makes me feel good to volunteer. What goes around comes around and I want this Christmas to be perfect for everyone," she said. "It's our first together."

"It's already perfect for me. Santa came early this year. I've already got everything I want." The depth of his feelings for this woman was right there in Forrest's eyes.

"Me, too." Angie leaned her head against his shoulder for a moment.

Shane felt like an intruder at the same time he envied them. *People Magazine*'s most eligible bachelor chef had never felt quite so alone before and he was sure that information would surprise the inquiring minds that wanted to know. It wasn't so much about this young couple as it was wanting to touch Gianna and not being able to. Denying himself the pleasure of kissing her under the stars seemed more than stupid when he looked at these two.

"Actually, Shane, I'm really glad they let you out of the kitchen tonight."

"It happens every once in a while." He grinned at them.

"We were hoping to see you," she said.

"Planning to hit me up to cater your wedding reception?" he teased.

"Maybe." Forrest laughed. "Seriously, we wanted to thank you again for all your hard work cooking such a fantastic Thanksgiving dinner for military families. Every single person said the only thing better would have been to have their son or daughter, father or mother home."

"He's right, Shane." Angie glanced at the man she loved, then back. "We can't thank you enough for what you did. You're the best."

"Not really."

He knew it was meant as a compliment but he wondered whether or not they'd feel the same if the truth came out that he was the son of Thunder Canyon's very own crook. He'd hurt Gianna tonight by brushing her off. If she knew the truth about him, she'd probably feel as if she'd dodged a bullet. Except for a strategically placed *R*, crook and cook were the same.

The burden of his father's identity still weighed heavily on him. For now it was his secret and keeping it to himself was the only way to control the flow of information. That meant not getting close to anyone.

Or kissing anyone. Immediately he thought of Gianna. Even her name sounded beautiful and exotic. The fire in her hair and freckles on her nose were a contradiction that tempted him every time he saw her.

And he saw her almost every day.

Chapter Three

At work on Friday Gianna was crabby and it was all Shane Roarke's fault. She'd seen him the previous night smiling his charming smile at the brunette and blonde, chatting them up as if they were the only two women in the world. That wouldn't bother her so much if he hadn't given her wine and food in this very kitchen and smiled his charming smile at *her*. Then he invited her to his place for a test run of a new recipe where he charmed her some more.

She loved being charmed but wished he'd kept it to himself because all of that attention had fed into her crush, the one now starved into submission because without fuel there was nowhere to go. She was doing her best to not think about him but that resolve was challenged earlier tonight when she'd seen him brooding. It was the same expression she'd noticed the night of her double duty, although what the handsome, successful, famous Shane Roarke had to brood about was beyond her.

She pushed through the double doors and he looked up from whatever he was sautéing. And that was the thing. He never looked up when he was cooking. The building could be on fire and he'd still focus on the food. A girl noticed stuff like that when she had a crush on a guy. For the last three days he'd ignored her unless special requests from a customer made a conversation necessary to get the order just right. Tonight Shane had looked at her every time she was around, no matter what he was doing.

Gianna ignored him as she put in the order for two salads with romaine lettuce and the most delicious croutons on the planet. The prep cook would toss it with Shane's special dressing, then add freshly grated Parmesan cheese. She picked up the wide, shallow bowls and set them on a tray. As she went to the double doors to go check on her tables a feeling prickled between her shoulder blades. Glancing over her shoulder she saw a hot and hungry expression in Shane's gaze. There was something up with him and she was involved.

As soon as she came back for the salads, she'd find out what was going on with him. After leaving the kitchen she walked through the maze of tables and stopped.

She knew these two, had seen them in here individually. Both were somewhere in their mid-fifties, and widowed. She saw they still had salad on the plates in front of them on the white, cloth-covered table. "Still working on those salads, Mrs. Bausch, Mr. Walters."

He was a big bear of a man with the calloused hands and leathery skin of someone who worked outdoors. "When are you going to call me Ben, little lady?"

"As soon as you stop calling me little lady. My name is Gianna."

"You got it, Gianna." There was a twinkle in his blue eyes.

"I haven't seen you two in here together before." She was curious.

"This is a blind date." Kay Bausch was characteristically direct. "Austin Anderson set us up. You probably know he's an engineer at Traub Oil Montana where I'm the secretary to the company president."

"Ethan?"

"Points to you, Gianna. That's the right Traub. And there are so many of them that sometimes it's hard to keep the names straight." She looked across the table at her blind date. "Ben has known him since he was a teenager. Austin, not Ethan."

"He's a good kid," Ben answered, his mouth curving upward to form a smile in his rugged face. "He was kind of lost after his mom died in a car accident when he was only a teenager. Turned out he just needed a steady hand."

"That's nice at any age." Kay's voice was a little wistful. "And now he's got his wife, Rose, Ethan's sister. They'll have their first anniversary on Christmas."

Gianna felt a twist in her chest that signaled a severe case of envy. She'd seen the couple in here for dinner and the glow of their love still radiated. It's what she had once hoped to find and now had all but given up on. Still, feeling sorry for herself was something she tried to do on her own time.

"Apparently Austin is quite the romantic."

"How do you mean?" Ben asked her, but the expression on his face said he knew where she was going with this.

"He fixed you two up. How's that working for you?" She looked at Kay, then Ben.

His grin was full of the devil. "So far I'm not sorry I put on this coat and tie."

"You look very handsome. And uncomfortable," Kay added. "The effort has not gone unnoticed or unappreciated."

"Good to know. Because it has to be said that there's no way to beat a comfortable pair of jeans."

"I couldn't agree more," his date said.

"Something in common already." Gianna nodded approvingly. "Can I get you anything else right now?"

"Nope. Got everything so far." Ben was looking at his companion, who smiled like a young girl.

"Okay, then. *Bon appétit.* You two enjoy."

Again weaving through the dining-room tables filled with people, she made her way back to the kitchen. Shane looked up as he was arranging shrimp in wine sauce over rice on two plates. Bonnie grabbed them, threw a nod of support, then left with the plates on a tray. She was alone with the chef and it was a sign, Gianna thought.

She marched over to where he stood in front of the stove and not all the heat she felt was from the cooking. "What's going on?"

"Excuse me?"

"Are you going to have me fired?" She folded her arms over her chest as she met his gaze. She didn't know where the question came from but her luck had been so bad it was best to get the worst case scenario out of the way first.

The surprise in his eyes was genuine. "What?"

"You keep staring at me and it's not a happy look. You're going to tell the manager to fire me, aren't you?"

"No."

She waited for an explanation, but it didn't come. "Then it's my imagination that you keep watching me?"

"No."

Again nothing further. He was the most frustrating, exasperating man she'd ever met and she had a talent for meeting exasperating men who frustrated her. "Then I don't get it. I don't understand what you want from me."

A muscle jerked in his jaw and his mouth pulled tight. He

was fighting some internal battle and it was anyone's guess which way things would go. Finally he all but growled, "Then I'll show you what I want."

He took her hand and tugged her down the short hallway and into the large, walk-in pantry where nonperishable, industrial-size supplies were kept. Canned goods, jars of olive oil, flour, sugar and spices were all stored in here on floor-to-ceiling metal shelves. Shane shut the door, closing them in.

"You know," Gianna said, her tone a little breathless, "you didn't need to bring me in here to yell at me. Public chastisement is okay. I can take it. Just tell me what—"

The words were cut off when he pulled her into his arms. "This is what I want to tell you."

And then he kissed her. His lips were soft, gentle, but there was nothing gentle about the effect on her senses. It felt as if a wave of emotions crashed over her and she was floating because her legs went weak. The scent of his spicy cologne mixed with the pleasant smell of oil, spices and fire. Blood pounded in her ears and the feel of her breasts crushed against his hard chest was simply scrumptious.

He cupped the back of her head in his palm to make the meeting of their mouths more firm, and the harsh sounds of his breathing combined with hers and filled the storeroom. She would have been happy to stay like that forever, but Shane pulled away. It could have been an hour or a nanosecond because time in this alternate sensuous universe was hard to quantify.

She blinked up at him and said, "Does that mean I'm not in trouble?"

"That's what it means." He leaned his forehead against hers. "I've been wanting to do that all week."

"Really?" Since her thoughts were smoking hot along with the rest of her, Gianna had trouble pulling herself together to call him on the fact that he'd ignored her most of the week. Somehow she managed. "You have a very odd way of showing it."

"You're right." He blew out a long breath and backed up a step, as if he needed distance to think clearly, too. "My behavior is inexcusable. Mixed signals."

"You think?"

"I don't think. It's a fact I've been running hot and cold."

"I noticed." After that kiss she definitely preferred hot, but given his recent mercurial moods it was best not to have expectations.

"Personal stuff in the workplace is a rocky road to go down. It's tricky to navigate. I was trying to take the high road, do the right thing. I'd never want to make you uncomfortable."

"You could have used your words," she pointed out, "said something. I know a thing or two about being conflicted regarding...personal stuff."

"Oh?"

"Yes." She lifted her chin a little self-consciously. In for a penny, in for a pound. Might as well use her words. Never let it be said she was a do-as-I-say-not-as-I-do person. "I understand how sometimes it's easy starting down a path, but the right time to turn off it can be tricky."

"Very Zen of you."

"Okay. Here's an example. I dated a divorce attorney for over two years before we had 'the talk' where I found out he never planned to commit. Should have turned off that path a lot sooner."

"I see."

"Then there was the accountant who saw too many joint checking accounts split, not necessarily down the middle, by messy breakups. There's a year and a half I'll never get back."

"Okay."

"The college professor who said up front that he was a loner. That one is my own fault."

"You've definitely had a conflict or two."

"Yes, I have. As with my job, I can handle it. You don't need to protect me. I'm a big girl."

"I noticed." His eyes were like twin blue flames with the heat turned up high.

"Don't hold back on my account."

"It won't happen again," he agreed.

"That was a very nice kiss."

One of his dark eyebrows lifted. "Nice?"

"Location, location, location." She looked around the storeroom and wrinkled her nose. "For the record? The balcony of your apartment has much better mojo."

"Everyone's a critic." He grinned. "Let me make it up to you."

"How?" She should be ashamed at being so easy, but darned if she could manage that.

"Meet me here after work and I'll show you."

"Okay." Way too easy. The end of her shift wouldn't come fast enough.

All it took was Shane's kiss to make her crabby mood disappear. Probably not smart, but definitely the truth.

After making sure everything in the kitchen was shut down and squared away to his satisfaction, Shane turned off the lights. Only the security ones were left on, making the interior dim. The frenzied chaos so much a part of the food-service business he loved was over for the night and eerie quiet took its place.

He waited for Gianna to get her coat and purse then meet him here. Keyed up from work, he paced while he waited. Part of him hoped she wouldn't show because he didn't need more complications in his life. Mostly he couldn't wait to see her. Fighting the temptation to kiss her had given him a lot of time to imagine what it would be like, but the actual touching of lips had been everything he'd expected and more.

What he hadn't expected was her straightforward sass and steadfast spunk. The way she'd challenged him about how peculiarly he'd been acting had surprised and charmed him in equal parts. He hadn't been surprised in a good way since the first time he'd seen Thunder Canyon.

With his parents' blessing, he'd hired a private investigator to find his biological parents and the guy had narrowed the search to this small town in nowhere, Montana. His restless need to connect the dots about himself had been stronger than his aversion to packing himself off to that small town. The surprise was his instant connection to the rugged beauty of the mountains and trees, being drawn in by the friendliness of the people.

He'd grown up in Los Angeles, for God's sake, where freeways, traffic and smog ruled. He wasn't a mountains-and-trees kind of guy. At least he'd never thought so. But the connection he'd felt had only gotten stronger in the five months he'd been here. That was already a lot to lose, and now there was Gianna.

That saying—the apple doesn't fall far from the tree— was a saying for a reason. And the sins of the father... The rest of the words eluded him but when sins were involved it couldn't be good. Something deep inside Shane rebelled at the thought of Gianna knowing who his father was.

The kitchen door opened and there she was, wearing a navy blue knit hat pulled over her red hair with curls peeking out by her collar. She had a matching scarf tied loosely around her neck and the ends dangled down the front of her coat. When she smiled, the beauty and warmth melted the place inside him that had started to freeze over.

"So," she said, "just how are you going to make it up to me?"

He wasn't quite sure, but when the moment was right, he'd know. "You'll just have to wait and see. Let's go."

"Okay."

There was a rear restaurant exit and she followed him past the pantry where he'd kissed her earlier and the big industrial-size refrigerator and freezer. He opened the outside door and let her precede him, then closed and locked it after them. The area was illuminated by floodlights at the corners of the building.

"That air feels so good," she said, drawing in a deep breath. "So clean and clear and cold."

"How do you feel about a midnight walk in the moonlight?"

Her blue eyes sparkled with merriment. "I feel like that's a promising start to making things up to me."

The restaurant employees parked here in the back and since they were the last two to leave, Shane figured the only car in the lot, an older model compact, belonged to Gianna.

He looked down at her. "You don't come out here alone after your shift, do you?"

"No. It usually works out that several of us leave together."

"Good." But tonight he would make sure she was safe. "Are you okay with leaving your car here?"

"Because someone might break in? I should be so lucky it would get stolen." She laughed and the cheerful sound magnified in the still night.

"Is it giving you trouble?"

"Trouble is too nice a word for what it gives me. Every

day I cross my fingers and say a little prayer that it will start and get me to work."

"If it ever doesn't, let me know. I can't afford to lose my best waitress."

"You might regret that offer," she warned.

They walked across the lot to the sidewalk that bordered an open grassy area. At least there used to be grass. He'd seen the green before winter rolled in and dumped a couple feet of snow. During the day the temperature was warm enough that the existing snow melted a little, wetting the walkway. The sun had gone down hours ago and it was freezing, making the sidewalk slippery. On top of that, a light snow had started to fall.

"So much for walking in the moonlight," she teased.

"I'm trying to feel bad about that. But for a boy from Southern California, the excitement of snow still hasn't worn off."

"All that sunshine and good weather must really get old."

"It's a dirty job, but someone has to live there."

She laughed. "Still, there's something to be said for Montana."

"Preaching to the choir, Gianna," he said. "And it's not just the landscape or weather. The people in this town are good, friendly, salt-of-the-earth types."

"I know what you mean." Her tone was serious and sincere. "I met people in New York. Still have a good friend there who used to be my roommate. But the city is so big and impersonal. There's an intimacy here that's unique."

"Everyone has made me feel really welcome, embraced me as one of them."

"Thunder Canyon spirit," she agreed. "But they can turn on you in a heartbeat if you let them down."

That's what worried him. But it probably wouldn't happen tonight. He made a deliberate decision to change the subject. "So, we had a pretty good crowd in the restaurant."

"We did." She glanced up at him. "Were you mad enough to spit when that man sent his steak back twice because it wasn't mooing on the plate?"

He shrugged. "People pay a lot of money for service and food. It's my job to make sure they're satisfied."

"For every persnickety person, there's a Ben Walters and Kay Bausch."

"I don't think I know them." When she slipped a little on the sidewalk, he took her hand and slid it through the bend of his elbow. It wasn't an excuse to stay connected. Not really. He was responsible for keeping her safe.

"Ben is in his mid-fifties, a rancher born and raised here. He's a widower. Kay is a transplant from Midland, Texas. She works for Ethan Traub and came with him when he opened Traub Oil Montana. She's a widow." She sighed. "I was their waitress tonight."

"Nice people?"

"Very. And the best part is they were on a blind date. Austin Anderson fixed them up."

"Angie's brother?"

"Yeah. It's really sweet. And I can't help wondering if the two of them were meant to meet and find a second chance at happiness. Romantic drivel, I know."

"Not here. To me it sounds like just another day in Thunder Canyon."

"On the surface that's sort of a cynical remark," she observed. "But digging deeper, I can see the compliment buried in the words."

They were walking by one of the resort's Christmas displays with lighted reindeer and Santa Claus in his sleigh. Animal heads moved back and forth and Rudolph's nose was bright red. The big guy with the white beard moved his hand in a wave. Old-fashioned, ornate streetlamps lined the walkways and the buildings were outlined with white lights.

"This is really a magical place, especially this time of year," he said.

"I know." There was a wistful tone to her voice as she stared at the decorations. "What is Santa bringing you this year? A Rolls Royce? 3-D TV with state-of-the-art sound system? Really expensive toys?"

Material things he had. And more money than he knew what to do with had paid for a private investigator to dig up information. But it was what money couldn't buy that made him feel so empty.

"I actually haven't written my letter to Santa yet."

"I see." She stared at the jolly fat man turning his head and waving. "Have you been naughty? Or nice?"

"Good question."

The mischief in her eyes turned his thoughts to other things and he looked at her mouth. The memory of those full lips so soft and giving convinced him that this was the right moment to make it up to her for not taking advantage of the romantic mojo on his balcony.

Shane lowered his head for a kiss, just the barest touch. He tasted strawberry lip gloss and snowflakes, the sexiest combination he could imagine. And he could imagine quite a bit. His heart rate kicked up and his breathing went right along with it. Gianna's did, too, judging by the white clouds billowing between them.

No part of their bodies were touching and she must have found that as dissatisfying as he did. She lifted her arms and put them around his neck, but when she moved, her foot slid on the sidewalk and she started to fall.

Shane shifted to catch her but couldn't get traction on the icy surface and knew both of them were going down. He managed to shift his body and take the brunt of the fall on his back in the snow while Gianna landed on top of him with a startled squeal. Then she started laughing.

He looked into her face so close to his and said, "That couldn't have gone better if I'd planned it." If he had, he'd have planned to be somewhere warm and for her not to have so many clothes on.

"So, you think it will be that easy to have your way with me?"

"A guy can hope."

Apparently the innocent expression he put on his face wasn't convincing because she chose that moment to rub a handful of snow over his cheeks.

He sucked in a breath. "God, that's cold."

"I'm so sorry." Clearly it was a lie because she did it again.

"Payback isn't pretty." He reached out to grab some snow, then lifted the collar of her coat to shove it down her back.

She shrieked again, then gave him a look. "You're so going down for that."

"I'm already down."

"Then we need to take this battle to a new level." She jumped up and staggered back a few feet, then bent down. When she straightened, she hurled a snowball with each hand, but missed him.

Shane rolled to the side and grabbed her legs, tackling her. "I learned to do that when I played football."

He looked down at her laughing face and thoughts of war and retaliation retreated. She was so beautiful he couldn't stop himself from touching his mouth to hers. Definitely going on Santa's naughty list this year.

He deepened the kiss and caught her moan of pleasure in his mouth as she slid her arms around his neck. They were already down so he didn't have to worry about losing his balance this time. That was fortunate because she felt so good in his arms, he had his doubts about maintaining emotional equilibrium.

He cupped her cold cheek in his palm and traced the outline of her lips with his tongue. She opened her mouth, inviting him inside, and he instantly complied. The touch sent liquid heat rolling through him and he groaned with the need to feel her bare skin next to his. The sensual haze lasted just until he felt her shiver.

He lifted his head and saw her shaking. "You're freezing."

"N-not yet. But c-close."

Shane levered himself up and to his feet, then reached a hand down to help her stand. In the streetlamp he could see that her coat and pants were wet. "You're soaked."

Her teeth were chattering, but she managed to say, "Th-thanks for the news flash."

"You need to get into something dry."

"I need to go h-home."

"My place is closer." The next words just popped out, but as soon as they did he knew how much he wanted it. "You could stay tonight."

"Oh, Shane—"

"Just a thought. No harm, no foul."

"I'd really like to." There was need in her eyes, but it was quickly followed by doubt. "But…"

There always was, he thought.

"I have an early day tomorrow," she said. "It's probably best if I go home. Rain check?"

"You got it." He'd never meant a promise more. "Now let's get you back to your car."

He hurried her to the parking lot and took her keys when her hand was shaking too badly to fit it in the lock. When she was in the driver's seat, she managed to get the key in the ignition and turn it. There was a clicking noise but the engine didn't turn over.

Shane met her gaze. "Did you forget to say your prayer this morning?"

"That's not the problem. This clunker is officially beyond the power of prayer. It's dead."

Chapter Four

Trouble wasn't a four-letter word but it should be when talking about her car, Gianna thought. On top of that, she was freezing. Rolling around in the snow with Shane had seemed like a good idea at the time, but not so much now.

He leaned into the open door and met her gaze. "I think the battery's dead."

"Of course it is because that's just how I roll—or in this case, don't roll. And dead is good."

"How do you figure?"

"It won't feel a thing when I beat it with a baseball bat."

"That won't help the situation."

"Says who? Hitting something would make me feel a lot better." She got out of the car, shivering when the cold air wrapped around her, then dug in her purse for her cell. "It's late. There's no way I can deal with this now. No garage will be open, so I'll call a cab to take me home."

He put a hand on her arm. "Not while I'm around."

"I don't want to inconvenience you."

If she'd taken him up on the offer to spend the night it would be very convenient, but she was pretty sure sleeping wasn't on his mind when he'd offered. It's not that she wasn't interested in sex, but this was too soon.

"I'm happy to help you out, Gianna. And I won't take no for an answer." He plucked his cell phone from the case on his belt, pushed some buttons and hit Send. A moment later he said, "Rob? Shane Roarke. Can you do me a favor? Bring my car down to the restaurant, the parking lot out back." Rob said something that made Shane grin. "Yes, a very nice Christmas bonus. Happy holidays." He put the phone back in the case. "The car will be here in a few minutes."

Gianna stared at him. "It must be amazing to be you."

"And who am I?" The words were meant to be glib and lighthearted but a slight tension in his voice made him sound a little lost.

Shane Roarke, celebrity chef and wealthy eligible bachelor? Lost? That was just nuts. She must have hit her head when they were wrestling in the snow. Or her brain was frozen. He was rich, famous, handsome. Women threw themselves at him. If this was a dream, she didn't want to wake up. And he was driving her home.

To her minuscule apartment above Real Vintage Cowboy. Yikes.

After seeing his place she was a little embarrassed to bring him inside hers. But that was just silly. After he pulled into the parking lot behind the store she'd just hop out and say thanks. There was no reason for him to know that her apartment was so small she could stand in the living room with a feather duster, turn once in a circle, and the place would be clean.

Headlights rounded the corner of the building then slowly

moved closer to them, finally stopping. A young man got out of the BMW SUV. "Here you go, Mr. Roarke."

"Thanks, Rob. Can I give you a lift back to the lobby?"

"No, thanks. The fresh air feels good, clears my head. That will help me stay awake and it's a long night ahead."

"Okay. Thanks again."

"Have a nice evening." He lifted his hand in a wave, then headed back the way he'd come.

"And just what is Rob's job title?"

"Concierge." He walked her to the passenger side of the car and opened the door. "One advantage of condo living is around-the-clock service."

"Does Rob's skill set lean toward replacing a dead car battery?" she wondered out loud.

"If you were one of my neighbors it would be his job to figure out how to do that."

"Rich people really are different."

He closed her door, walked around the front of the car and passed through the headlights, then slid in on the driver's side. "Where to?"

"Real Vintage Cowboy. It's on Main Street near the Wander-On Inn and Second Chances Thrift Store."

"I've been there. Isn't it closed this time of night?" He glanced over at her, questions and something else swirling in his eyes before he put the car in gear and drove out of the parking lot.

"My apartment is above the store. So you've been there?"

"Yes." Again his voice was tense. "I actually went shopping there. And for the record, rich people aren't different. I put my pants on one leg at a time."

"Okay. If you want to split hairs, I'll play," she said. "Have you ever been in the grocery store?"

"Here in Thunder Canyon, or ever?"

"Let's get wild. Here in town."

"No. I leave a list for the housekeeper."

"Of course you do." While he drove, she settled into the soft leather of the heated seat. Because Rob was Rob, he'd turned on the heater and the interior was warm in addition to feeling like a spaceship with all the dials and doohickeys on the dashboard. "I want a housekeeper and a Rob," she said wistfully.

"With great privilege comes great responsibility."

"Confucius says…" She glanced over at him, the rugged profile, the strong jaw and stubborn chin. There was something so appealing in his smile, a quality that tugged at her, made her want to touch him. "Would you translate that for me?"

"It means that money is a reward for hard work. A benefit of having it is being able to hire help so that when you're not working, complete relaxation is possible."

"So, getting into the milieu of my car, your batteries are recharged and you can go to work with renewed energy and make gobs more money."

There was irony in the glance he slid to her. "Something like that."

From where she was sitting, the rich were different, no matter what he said. That didn't mean their houses wouldn't burn in a wind-driven brush fire or their cars didn't break down. But when bad stuff happened there were no worries about the cost of fixing it. And you could hire someone to change a battery or flat without batting an eye.

Gianna would bet everything she had that the actresses, models and famous-for-being-famous women he dated wouldn't be fretting about how they were getting to work in order to earn the money to buy a car battery for a clunker. It was too depressing so she decided to change the subject.

"So, when you went to Real Vintage Cowboy, what were you shopping for?"

"I'm building a house."

That wasn't really an answer. "I heard a rumor to that effect. People talk about you."

"Because I'm different?"

"No. Because you're a celebrity." When the car stopped at a stoplight under a streetlamp, she saw the muscle in his jaw tighten. "So, because of the house-building rumor, I was a little surprised when you said you might not be renewing your contract at The Gallatin Room."

"All I did was confirm that it's only six months."

"Again you're splitting hairs." Now that she thought about it, he was pretty stingy with personal information. "If you're not staying, why build a house?"

"I found a great piece of land that was begging to be developed."

So, of course, he bought it and did just that, even though his time in Thunder Canyon might be limited. So much for his assertion that the rich weren't different. She thought about using what he'd just told her as evidence to support her statement, but decided against it. He would never understand.

The windshield wipers rhythmically brushed snow away as the car glided smoothly along nearly deserted Main Street. When they drove past The Hitching Post, Gianna tensed. The new and improved bar and restaurant had been thoroughly overhauled by new owner, Jason Traub. He'd managed to respect its Montana history and maintain the Western style while using reclaimed lumber and stones.

The upstairs, which used to be rooms for rent, had been converted into an intimate salon with overstuffed leather chairs, hand-carved rockers and antlers that hung on the wall. A large stone fireplace and cozy floor rugs made it a welcoming place for a quiet drink and conversation. None of that is what made her nervous.

A minute or two after going by, Shane turned the car into the lot behind Real Vintage Cowboy and pulled into a parking space closest to the building.

"Thanks a lot, Shane. I don't want to keep you." She started to open the passenger door.

"Let me turn the car off."

"Don't bother. You don't have to see me to my door. I'll just run upstairs. You've done enough already."

Her effort to make a smooth exit was wasted and she knew it when the car's dashboard lights revealed his amusement.

"If I didn't know better, I'd think you were nervous about something."

Not something, everything, she thought. "Not at all. I just don't want to take advantage of your kindness."

"Oh, please." He turned off the engine. "I'm not in the habit of barely slowing down to let a lady out of my car. Just so we're clear, I'm walking you to your door. No argument."

He'd left her no graceful way out of this and did it in such a gentlemanly way. Could be because he didn't know her very well and was on his best behavior. Could be an act meant to disarm her. If so, it was working. She was almost completely disarmed.

"Okay," she said. "But you should know. My apartment is on the third floor."

"Real men don't flinch at a second set of stairs."

"Don't say I didn't warn you."

Shane came around and opened her door, then walked beside her to the wooden stairs on the outside of the building. When they got to the landing, Gianna had her keys out. "Thanks, Shane. I had a great time tonight."

"Me, too." His gaze searched hers. "Did I redeem myself for first-kiss faux pas?"

She laughed. "Yeah."

"Good. Here's another better first."

He lowered his mouth to hers. It was soft and warm where their lips met, but the breeze swirled snow around them and made her shiver.

Instantly he pulled back. "I'm an idiot. Your clothes are still wet, aren't they?"

"Y-yes."

"You need to get inside. Good night, Gianna."

She nodded, but as he started to back away it hit her that she really didn't want him to go. A third kiss didn't mean she'd known him any longer, just convinced her that she wanted to spend more time with him. It wasn't smart, but the words came out of her mouth, anyway.

"You're cold, too. How about a cup of tea?"

"I wouldn't mind." He stared down at her, questions in his eyes. "But only if you're sure it's not too late. You've got stuff to do tomorrow."

His hand was on her arm; his gaze held hers. She was definitely sure. "It's not too late." Or maybe it was. "Just don't expect much. My apartment is nothing like your place."

Gianna unlocked the door and he followed her inside. She tried to tell herself that the actresses, models and TV personalities he dated probably had places this small but it didn't work.

The apartment was long, narrow and divided into two spaces—living room and kitchen, bedroom and bath. There was a window looking out on Main Street and the other faced the parking lot with rugged, majestic mountains in the distance. When you thought about it, she and Shane sort of shared a scenic view, but his was way better.

She'd separated her cooking and eating area with a hunter-green love seat. Braided rugs in green, coral and yellow were scattered over the wooden floor. The walls were painted a pale gold and had white baseboards and crown molding. Scattered pictures hung in groupings, a lot of them framed in cherrywood ovals. To shake things up, she'd put a two-foot section of a scaled-down ladder over the outside door and a hanging fixture over the stove held several copper pots and an orange colander. It was bright and cheerful, in her opinion.

She watched Shane, trying to gauge his reaction. "Be it ever so humble..."

"Have you ever heard the expression, 'it's not the square footage, but what you do with it'?"

She tapped her lip. "Is that like 'size doesn't matter'?"

"In a way." His grin was wicked and exciting. "You've created a space that's homey, comfortable and charming. A reflection of its occupant."

"So, let me see if I understand what you're saying. I'm homey and comfortable?"

"Don't forget charming," he said, looking around again, then coming back to meet her gaze. "Among other very attractive attributes. My place doesn't have this warmth..." He stopped. "And speaking of that, I'm an idiot. Get out of those damp clothes into something warm."

Your arms would be warm.

Gianna hoped she hadn't said that out loud and when his expression didn't change, she breathed a sigh of relief. "Okay. Let me get tea first—"

"I'll do it."

"But..."

"Do you have tea bags?" he asked.

"In the appropriately marked canister by the stove. It won't take a minute—"

"You don't trust me?" He shook his head. "I'm CIA. My culinary genius is the stuff of legend."

"Humble, too," she muttered.

"I think I can handle putting a couple of mugs with water in the microwave."

"Okay, then. Knock yourself out."

She walked through the doorway that separated the living room from her bedroom and bath. After closing the door, she stripped off her coat followed by the rest of her wet clothes. Still chilled to the bone, fashion and seduction were not her priority now. She pulled a pair of fleecy Santa Claus pants from her dresser and a green thermal shirt and put them on, then slipped into her oversize dark blue terrycloth robe, thick socks and fuzzy slippers.

In the adjoining bathroom she turned on the light and recoiled from her reflection in the mirror. "Oh, dear God."

Mascara from the lower lashes gave her "raccoon" eyes and her hair looked like she'd combed it with a tree branch. After washing her face to remove the makeup and free her freckles, she applied cream and ran a brush through her red hair. The cut that had layers falling past her shoulders was good, the color—not so much.

She was finally warm thanks to Shane getting her home as fast as possible. Inviting him in was equal parts boldness and stupidity. Conventional-dating protocol dictated three dates before sleeping with someone. Between dinner at his place and tonight's walk in the snow, they were barely at one.

She had no illusions about a future with Shane Roarke because he'd been honest about his uncertain plans. Still, she wanted him. That was the downside of giving him a first kiss do-over. The touch of his lips, the feel of his hard body pressed against hers had just made her want him even more.

And that was the stupid part of giving in to her boldness. Her heart was telling her to slow down; her head was saying take me now.

There was very little danger of him doing that, she

thought, looking at her reflection. The old robe and Christmas pants would prove to the seduction police that she hadn't dressed to lure him to her bed.

"You're comfortable and homey, the complete opposite of a temptress," she said to herself. "Charming is debatable."

With a sigh she opened the door and joined him in the kitchen. "I see you found everything."

"Yes." He'd removed his coat and settled it on the standing rack by the front door. Now he was leaning against the counter with two steaming mugs beside him. His jeans were fashionably worn and fit his lean legs perfectly. The white cotton shirt fit his upper body in the most masculine way. But what hiked up her pulse was the amusement in his eyes as his gaze scanned her from head to toe. "Love the outfit."

Looking down she said, "I'll start a new fashion trend. Montana practical."

"I think you look pretty cute." He traced a finger across her cheek. "Love the freckles."

"Yeah." She wrinkled her nose distastefully. "Me, too."

"What's wrong with them?"

"When I was in grade school, the boys wanted to play connect the dots on my face. That got really old. The curse of a redhead."

"Your hair is beautiful and unique."

"I always wanted to be a blonde or brunette."

"Boring."

The simple, straightforward word warmed her the way fleece, thermal and terrycloth never could. "Still, there's something to be said for blending in. Being different made me a target of teasing."

"It's a well-known fact that boys are stupid."

"You'll get no argument from me." She raised her gaze to find him watching her and a sizzle of awareness sprinted down her spine. When he moved closer, her heart started to pound.

"But we get smarter." He cupped her face in his hands and slid his lips over her cheek, soft nibbling kisses that made drawing air into her lungs a challenge. "How's that for connecting the dots?"

"Great technique." Her voice was a breathless whisper and she felt his lips curve into a smile. The only thing that would make this better was his mouth on hers. "Definitely smarter."

"But wait. There's more," he said a little hoarsely.

Gianna pressed her palm to his chest and felt the heavy beat of his heart then shivered at the heat in his gaze. "More sounds good to me."

Strangely enough she didn't agonize over the right or wrong of this. It just was. She wanted him, wanted to give herself to him. No questions; no regrets.

She felt his hand loosen the belt of her robe and slide inside, cup her hip. The good thing about oversize clothing was how easily you could slip it off.

When their gazes locked, she saw invitation in the smoldering depths darkening his blue eyes. "Do you want to see the bedroom?"

"Only if you want to show it to me."

Her answer was to take his hand and lead him through the doorway. The light beside the bed was on, illuminating her simple, white chenille spread. Throw pillows in light pink and rose gave it color, but she threw them onto the floor. Shane was the only man she'd ever brought in here and he seemed to fill the room, complete it somehow.

Gianna folded down the bedspread and blanket, revealing her serviceable flannel sheets. "Not sexy, just practical for a Montana winter. Otherwise I scream like a woman when I go to bed."

One of his dark eyebrows rose as his mouth curved into a wicked grin. "There's nothing wrong with screaming like a woman."

"I agree—when it's not from cold sheets."

"I promise you won't be cold." He traced his index finger along her collarbone and proved the truth of those words.

Shards of heat burned through her, warming her everywhere. Her toes curled and she stepped out of her slippers. But she hadn't let him be the first man in this room just to be a passive participant. She tugged his shirt from the waistband of his jeans and started undoing its buttons. Then she pressed her palms to his bare chest, letting the dusting of hair scrape across her hands, the nerve endings in her fingers.

The moan that built inside her refused to stay contained and Shane took it from there. He shrugged out of his shirt, then took the hem of hers and lifted it over her head.

He cupped her bare breasts and brushed his thumbs over the soft skin. "Beautiful."

She put her hands over his knuckles and gently pressed, showing him without words how perfect it felt. His breathing increased and the harsh sound of it mingled with hers. The scent of him, the heat of his skin, the feel of his hands all capsized her senses and drowned her in need. She backed toward the mattress and tugged him with her. Then she pushed off her fleece Santa pants and toed off her socks. His eyes darkened with approval and the heat of desire.

Gianna sat on the bed and even though the flannel sheets were cold on her bare skin, there was no screaming. Just acute anticipation. She watched Shane unbuckle his belt and step out of his jeans, then pull a condom from his wallet and set it on the nightstand. She wasn't sure he could see it in her eyes, but she most definitely approved. His shoulders were wide, his belly flat, his legs muscular. He was fit and fine and—for tonight—hers.

She held out her arms and he came into them, pressing her back on the mattress. He kissed her deeply and she opened, letting him stroke the inside of her mouth. While he ravaged her there, he slid a hand down her waist and belly, then her inner thigh. The touch tapped into a mother lode of desire and she could hardly breathe.

"Oh, Shane, I want—"

"I know."

He reached for the condom and covered himself, then rolled over her, between her legs, taking most of his weight on his forearms. Slowly he entered, filling her fully, sweetly. Her hips arched upward, showing him, urging him.

She could hardly draw enough air into her lungs as he stroked in and out with exquisite care. Then he reached between their bodies and brushed his thumb over the bundle of nerve endings at the juncture of her thighs.

The touch pushed her over the edge where she shattered into a thousand pieces. Shane held her and crooned words that her pleasure-saturated mind couldn't comprehend but knew were just right.

As if he knew the perfect moment, he started to move again. His breathing grew more ragged until there was one final thrust and he went still, groaning out his own release. Like he'd done for her, she wrapped her arms around him and just held on.

"Gianna—" Her name was a caress riding on a satisfied sigh.

"For the record—" She kissed his chin and the sexy scruff scraped her passion swollen lips in the nicest possible way.

"Yes," he urged.

"Boys really do get smarter."

She felt the laugh vibrate through his chest where their bare skin touched. Ordinarily that would have made her smile, but she couldn't quite manage. Boys might be smarter, but girls were notorious for making stupid choices. She had the emotional scars to prove she'd made the same ones multiple times.

She just hoped this wasn't a different kind of mistake, the kind that would make her sorry in the morning.

Chapter Five

Shane woke when Gianna mumbled in her sleep and moved restlessly against him. They were spooning, a term he used in cooking but liked a whole lot better in this context. If finding out his biological father was a criminal in jail was the worst thing since coming to Thunder Canyon, this was the best. He nuzzled her silky red hair and grinned.

Light was just beginning to creep into the room around the edges of the white blinds over the window and the number on the clock by the bed made him groan. Because his business was primarily done in the evening, he always slept in. His day usually started much later than this, but he had to admit it had never started better.

Gianna stretched sleepily then went still after her legs brushed against his. Without looking over her shoulder she asked, "Shane?"

"You were expecting someone else?"

"No." She cuddled into him. "I was sure I'd dreamed last night."

"A nightmare?"

"Oh, please. It was wonderful and you're very aware of that. I refuse to feed your ego."

"Then how about feeding me some breakfast?"

"I'll try. After I throw on some clothes. Meet you in the kitchen. Five minutes. I get the bathroom first."

Before he could ask a question or form any sort of protest, she'd thrown back the covers and raced from the bed. While waiting his turn, Shane thought about the situation. Sex was a very efficient recipe for stress relief and his body was really relaxed for the first time in longer than he could remember. That's not to say he hadn't been with women, but the vibe was different with Gianna.

Maybe it was more intense because their time together would be short. She wasn't staying and if information came out about who he really was, he wouldn't have to make a choice about his contract since it wouldn't be renewed. All he knew for sure was that as long as the two of them were in town, he wanted to see her.

Within the designated time frame, he joined her in the kitchen. She was wearing the same fleece pants, thermal top and robe from last night, which was both good and bad. She looked every bit as cute and he wanted to take the clothes off her again.

"Coffee?" She stood in front of the machine on the counter and glanced over her shoulder. When she met his gaze, a lovely blush stole over her cheeks as if she knew what he'd been thinking.

"I'd love it," he said.

"Coming right up." She added water, then put a filter and grounds in the appropriate place before pushing the start button.

"What did you mean about trying to feed me breakfast?"

"I'm not sure what I've got to cook," she explained.

"Let me have a look."

"Be my guest." She laughed. "Oh. Wait. You are my guest. And I'm the worst hostess on the planet if I let you do the cooking. There just may not be much in the refrigerator."

He slid her a wry look. "I won a reality cooking show by whipping up a gourmet meal with jelly beans, popcorn, granola, shrimp and instant mashed potatoes."

"Let me just say—eww." She folded her arms over her chest. "But far be it from me to stand in your way. Go to it, chef boy."

He lifted one eyebrow. "You do remember I'm the boss?"

"Not right now, you're not," she shot back. "At this moment you're my—guy in the kitchen."

"Good to know. Let's see what guy-in-the-kitchen has to work with."

The contents of her pantry and refrigerator were limited. It was the female equivalent of a bachelor's. Half a bottle of white wine. He grabbed the open milk container and took a sniff that told him it was still good. Individually wrapped slices of cheese. A couple of limp celery stalks and a few green onions. There was a loaf of bread touting fiber, low calories and weight control. Thank God she had half a dozen eggs.

He pulled the ingredients out and set to work with the cutting board, frying pan and a silent, solemn promise to equip her kitchen better. Starting with a decent set of knives.

He held up an old, dull one. "This is where it all starts. I recommend high carbon, stainless steel. It's the best of both worlds. Carbon is tough and has a great edge. Stainless steel keeps it from rusting and taking care of it is a lot less effort."

"Good to know. Can I do anything besides an emergency run to the kitchen gadget store?" she asked.

"Set the table and stay back."

Not that he couldn't work with her underfoot. The Gallatin Room kitchen was always swarming with people, a well-choreographed cauldron of activity, but experience had taught him how to tune everything out. He'd only ever been unsuccessful at doing that when Gianna was around.

He glanced at her in that oddly sexy oversize robe and felt his blood heat like butter in a frying pan. Now that he'd explored the curves under her quirky outfit, if she got any closer to him, resisting her would annihilate his concentration.

Fifteen minutes later they sat at her dinette just big enough for two and ate toast, cheese omelets and coffee. Gianna took a bite and made a sexy little sound of appreciation, not unlike something he'd coaxed from her in bed.

"This is so good, Shane."

"You sound surprised."

"Not at you. Just that it was possible from my survival rations." She chewed another bite. "Mmm. I can only imagine what you could whip up after a trip to the market."

Which reminded him... The reason they were here and not at his place was because she had an early day.

"So, you're up before God," he said. "What's on your agenda today?"

"I have to start my Christmas shopping."

"Really? By yourself?"

"Unlike the great and powerful Shane Roarke I don't have minions to do it for me."

"That's a shame."

"No kidding."

"Want some help?" He wasn't a fan of shopping but he was becoming a fan of Gianna's. He wanted to hang out with her even if that involved poking through stores and carrying bags. "I could be your minion."

"Singular?" Her auburn eyebrow lifted slightly. "By definition doesn't minion mean more than one?"

"How about if I chauffeur? Then it would be me and the car."

"Oh, gosh, I forgot. What with us— After we— Well, you know." She looked at him, blushing like crazy. "My car died last night."

He'd never heard sex described as us, we and you know, but definitely understood how it could push everything else from one's mind.

"Since you don't have wheels, that's even more reason to let me come along. I'll make a phone call and have the local garage bring your car back from the dead while you take care of Christmas." Sipping coffee, he watched her mull it over. "Gianna?"

"Hmm?"

"Don't think it to death. Just say yes. It's a good offer."

"It's an outstanding offer and I'd be all kinds of crazy to turn it down. Thank you, Shane." She stood and leaned over the small table to kiss his cheek. "My hero."

Right now, maybe. For as long as she didn't know the identity of his father. And there was no reason she should, even if he actually found out who his mother was. Right now all he knew was her first name. Grace.

A problem for another day. At this moment Gianna was looking at him as if he had wings and a halo. It felt really good and he didn't want that to change. Keeping his secret was the best way to do that.

Gianna was rocking a pretty awesome post-sex, post-breakfast glow while she waited for Shane to pick her up. She was scouting out Real Vintage Cowboy, the shop below her apartment, which was where they'd agreed to meet after he went home to shower and change.

There was a Christmas tree in the window decorated with ornaments made out of clothespins fashioned into reindeer, beads strung together into snowflakes, crystal dangles from old lamps and tin Santas and sleighs. Meandering the main aisle, she admired a saddle lovingly repaired and polished, a turn-of-the-century, repainted Singer sewing machine and a milk can holding a lamp as an example of how it could be used as an end table.

Everything looked beautiful to her this morning. She was happy. Being with Shane was magic and something about eating breakfast together was more intimate than sex. Her world was bright with possibilities and she believed with every fiber of her being that it really was the most wonderful time of the year.

Catherine Clifton Overton was standing by the far wall, near the cash register. She saw Gianna and smiled. "Hey, tenant."

"Merry Christmas, landlady."

The woman she paid her rent to was a willowy brunette with the warmest, darkest chocolate-colored eyes Gianna had ever seen. She was wearing a turtleneck top that came down over her hips and a coordinating gauzy skirt that skimmed the top of her signature cowboy boots. A leather belt cinched her small waist and pulled the whole outfit together perfectly.

Gianna's style leaned more to black-black jeans, gray sweater, black boots, leftovers from her days in New York. Compared to her landlady she felt as if she was on the fashion police's most wanted list.

"So how's married life?" she asked.

"Absolutely perfect." Catherine had a dreamy expression

on her face as she glanced at the wedding and engagement rings on her left hand. "Cody makes me so happy."

"You're a lucky woman. I envy you." Gianna figured if she couldn't stop the stab of jealousy, it was best to be up-front about it. "He's a great guy."

At this point in her life she'd expected to have what Catherine did—a growing business and marriage to the man of her dreams. She was a failure on both counts. As she saw it, the lesson was to not have expectations. Take it one day at a time. And today she was going to be happy.

Just then the bell over the front door rang and in walked Shane Roarke.

"Speaking of great guys…" Catherine arched an eyebrow. "I wonder what he's looking for this time."

"He told me about checking out your store." Gianna waved at him and he started toward her across the long room.

The other woman lowered her voice. "He was browsing and we ended up talking. He had a lot of questions about Arthur Swinton and the last owner of this place."

"Jasper Fowler?" Gianna had heard about the crazy old man who had conspired with Swinton to steal money and ruin the Traub family. The two were currently in jail.

Catherine whispered. "Vintage items all have a story. Shane just might be a man who appreciates that."

That implied he had a story, but Gianna was more interested in admiring the man. More caught up in the way her heart skipped and her breath caught at the sight of him. The broad shoulders and long legs wrapped in designer jeans would make it easy to mistake him for a cowboy. This was Montana after all, a little off the beaten path for a celebrity chef.

He walked up beside her and smiled at Catherine. "Nice to see you again."

"Same here. Can I help you find something?"

"I just did."

Gianna shivered at the sparkle in his eyes when she met his gaze. "My car is being uncooperative, as usual. Shane volunteered to take me Christmas shopping."

"Really?" Catherine looked impressed. And curious. What woman wouldn't be? "Most guys would rather take a sharp stick in the eye."

"I guess I'm not most guys." He grinned at them.

"My husband could take lessons from you."

"Didn't you just tell me he's perfect?" Gianna said.

"In most ways," the other woman agreed. "But, like the average man, he's a little shopping-challenged."

"I never said I'd be good at it," Shane corrected. "Just promised to do the driving."

Catherine tapped her lip as she studied him. "Do you give cooking lessons? Maybe I could persuade you to teach my husband a couple easy recipes."

"I'm happy to help out." He looked at Gianna. "Speaking of helping, I made a phone call. The garage is working on fixing your car as we speak and it will be delivered back here today. They're going to leave the keys with you, Catherine, if we're not back. Is that okay?"

"Of course. And in the spirit of good deeds—" she looked from him to Gianna "—do you know about Presents for Patriots?"

"I've already signed up to volunteer," Gianna answered, knowing what was coming. "Most of The Gallatin Room employees have."

"I haven't heard about this," Shane said.

"That's because you're not an employee," she shot back. "You're the boss."

"What is it?"

"Last year," Catherine said, "people in town got together

and wrapped donated gifts for military personnel serving overseas who couldn't get home for Christmas."

Shane nodded approvingly. "Sounds like a terrific event."

"You should come by if you're not too busy," the other woman suggested.

"I will. Where?"

"The Rib Shack. It's D. J. Traub's pet project." Maybe it was from working around things that all had a story, but Catherine warmed to telling one. "His mother, Grace, died when he was just a boy and he had difficulty connecting with his dad. They reconciled before Doug Traub died, but because of what he went through, family is very important to him."

"Okay."

It was one word, but Gianna heard something in Shane's voice and looked at him. His easygoing, relaxed manner had disappeared and there was tension in his jaw.

Catherine didn't seem to notice. "D.J. feels that we're all part of the American family and the military fights to preserve that for us. Presents for Patriots is his way of giving back to them for all they do."

"A worthy cause." Shane looked down at her. "Are you ready to go?"

"Actually, yes. There's a lot to do and a limited amount of time to do it in. Yesterday I made a date to meet my mother and sister for a late lunch. You're welcome to join us if you have time."

"Then we should get started." Shane didn't accept or decline, but put his hand on her lower back, a courtly gesture except she could feel him urging her to leave. "Have a good day, Catherine."

"You, too." She smiled. "Or just grit your teeth and get through it."

As they headed for the door Gianna didn't feel ready

for this expedition at all. It was possible she'd imagined the shift in Shane's mood, but not likely. The contrast was too stark. He'd arrived and was his usual friendly, charming self. When the subject of volunteering came up, he'd turned dark and broody. What was up with that?

Envying Catherine Overton hadn't punctured her happy balloon, but an "aha" moment did the trick. She'd slept with this man less than twelve hours before but still didn't really know very much about him.

Shane's SUV was at the curb in front of Real Vintage Cowboy and he held the door open for her. She could feel his body language change as soon as they walked outside. He was more relaxed, which made her think whatever had brought on the mood was somehow connected to Catherine or the store. Gianna slid into the car and couldn't contain a small sigh of pleasure as her body connected with the butter-soft leather.

When he was in the driver's seat, engine on and purring, Shane said, "Where to?"

Gianna returned his smile and pulled the list out of her purse. "Mountain Bluebell Bakery. It's at the corner of Nugget and Main in Old Town. Just east of the Tottering Teapot and ROOTS."

"Got it."

He put the car in gear, then glanced over his left shoulder before easing out into the stream of light traffic. Only the drifts of snow still in the shade were evidence of last night's storm. The street was clear, the sky was blue and the bad vibe was behind them.

"So, on this shopping expedition, I'm surprised the Bakery is the first stop. You've got a sweet tooth all of a sudden? Need an energy boost so you can shop till you drop? Or is there something I need to know?"

"Only that you should be warned. This will probably be

the easiest shopping of the day. I'm ordering something to send to a friend in New York."

"Male or female?" he asked.

"What?" She looked at him, the chiseled profile that made her want to touch his face.

"Your friend in New York. Man or woman?"

His tone was just a little too casual and that made her happy. "Before I answer that, I have a question."

"Okay."

"Are you jealous?"

He glanced at her and before returning his gaze to the road, his eyes burned bright and hot. "No. Just making conversation."

She was pretty sure that was a lie and a little ball of pleasure bumped against her heart. "Then, in the spirit of conversation…my friend is a woman. Hannah Cummings. We were roommates before I moved back to Thunder Canyon. I'm trying to talk her into coming for a visit."

"Will you be here that long?"

"My plans are still up in the air." That was true. She still hadn't fine-tuned her Plan B. Before he could question her more, the bakery came into view. "There it is. Looks like there's a parking place out front."

"I see it."

"That's really lucky. Lizzie Traub opened it about a year ago and this place is always busy." She chattered away. "She got some great publicity when the former owner, who was going to make Corey and Erin Traub's wedding cake, closed the place and left town with people's deposits. Lizzie made their cake and saved the wedding day."

"Is Corey related to D.J.?"

"They're cousins," she answered. "Lizzie and Ethan weren't married then. She was his administrative assistant and relocated to Thunder Canyon from Midland, Texas. Her family's bakery was a landmark there for years until her father lost money and the bank repossessed it."

"How do you know all this?" There was no teasing in his voice, just awe. "Weren't you living in New York?"

She didn't like reminders of her failed life. "My mother and sister live here. They talk to me."

"I'll keep that in mind," he said, pulling to a stop in front of the shop.

They got out of the car, walked inside and were immediately surrounded by the sweet smells of chocolate and icing. Gianna could almost feel her pores absorbing the sugar and calories and couldn't find the will to care. Her mouth was watering and she wasn't even hungry.

One glass case was filled with muffins—blueberry, pumpkin spice, banana nut, chocolate chip and more. Another display had old-fashioned donuts and buttermilk bars. Yet another showed cupcakes and specialty cakes and a book filled with pictures from various events handled by Mountain Bluebell Bakery.

A tall, beautiful woman in her twenties with gray-green eyes and dark blond hair walked out of the back room. "Hi. I'm Lizzie Traub."

"Nice to meet you. Gianna Garrison," she said and held out her hand. "And this is Shane Roarke."

"The chef at The Gallatin Room. I never missed your show—*If You Can't Stand the Heat.* You really smoked the competition. Pun intended." Lizzie smiled.

"Thanks." He grinned at her, then looked around at the bakery's interior. "I defy anyone to be gloomy in here."

"I like bright colors and since I spend a lot of time working, it seemed wise."

The shop was cheerful and bright with signs advertising Wi-Fi and tables scattered over the floor. It was the kind of place where someone could come for an espresso and muffin, set up a laptop and stay for a while. There were café lights with blown glass shades swirling with orange, yellow and blue, a sampling of the color scheme. Three walls were painted a sunny yellow and the long one behind the counter was a rich, deep burnt umber. At waist level along each wall flowed an endless chain of mountain bluebells.

"I love what you've done with the place. I hear the guy who used to own it wasn't nice, not a bluebells-on-the-walls type," Gianna commented.

"Tell me about it." Lizzie looked at the flowers. "My friend Allaire Traub hand stenciled all of that. She's so talented and great with kids. She teaches art at the high school."

"You could hate someone like that if they weren't so nice," Gianna said.

"I know, right?" Lizzie looked from one to the other. "Can I help you with something?"

"My sister highly recommended you. Jackie Blake?"

"Right." Lizzie nodded. "Three kids—Griffin, Colin and Emily. All chocolate connoisseurs, although they love the Mountain Bluebell muffins, too."

"That sounds like my niece and nephews."

"Adorable children." She smiled at Shane, then said, "But I have to say that I'm feeling some pressure. Your Gallatin Room desserts are legendary."

He smiled. "I fill a completely different business niche. And from what I see, your product is amazing."

"Thanks." She looked at each of them. "So, what can I help you with?"

"I understand that you ship orders?"

Lizzie nodded. "Anything over fifty dollars is no charge for shipping and handling. And I guarantee it will get there fresh."

"That sounds perfect."

"Did you want to sample something?"

"More than you can possibly imagine, but I already know what I want." She pointed into the display case. "Red velvet cupcakes."

"For Christmas, I assume?" At her nod, Lizzie continued. "Maybe a reindeer or Santa on the icing? Like the ones in the case."

Gianna bent to look. "Very festive. Sold."

"Wow." Shane looked impressed. "A woman who knows her mind."

It took a few minutes to fill out an order form with her choice, the quantity and the address in New York. When there was a total, Gianna handed over her credit card, then signed the receipt.

"Thanks, Lizzie. That was quick and I'm crunched for time."

"You made it easy."

Shane laughed. "She told me this would be the easiest errand of the day."

"I'm glad she was right. Come back again."

"Definitely."

They walked back outside and Gianna pulled her list out of her purse, then checked off the first item. "That's one down. Now there's my mom and dad. Jackie and her husband and my nephews and niece. A little something for Bonnie. I'm thinking maybe the mall would be good, going for a variety of stores rather than a lot of separate stops. But I'm feeling a little guilty about monopolizing your time."

"You shouldn't," he said. "I don't mind."

"Do you need to do some shopping for your family?" She looked up at his dark aviator sunglasses that hid his eyes. It occurred to her again that she knew very little about him. He'd never said much about himself. "I'm assuming you weren't raised by wolves."

"My mom and dad live in Los Angeles."

"Any siblings?" she asked, noting the dark change in tone and the way his mouth tightened.

"A sister and brother." He started to take her elbow and lead her to the car. "Next stop New Town Mall."

There was something going on with him. That was twice in less than an hour that he'd gone weird on her. If there was a problem she needed to know now. Relationships that had gone on too long had taught her not to ignore signs of trouble.

She dug in her heels. "Wait, Shane."

"What's wrong?"

"That's what I want to know." She looked up at him, took a deep breath and said, "I know you're struggling with something today. What's going on? Is it us? Are you sorry about last night?"

Chapter Six

"God, no."

Shane was sorry about a lot of things and right at the top of the list was the man who'd fathered him. But he would never in a million years regret being with Gianna. It was wonderful. She was amazing.

Standing on the sidewalk outside the Mountain Bluebell Bakery he looked into her eyes. "Last night was the best. And now who's feeding whose ego—"

She smiled as intended, but there was still concern in her beautiful turquoisey eyes. "Then what is it?"

He really thought he'd done a pretty good job of hiding his feelings. First when Catherine Overton had mentioned D. J. Traub's mother. It was the first time he'd heard her name. Grace was his birth mother's name, too. And just now when Gianna had asked him about his family, he was reminded that he was here in Thunder Canyon to dig up information about who he was. That thought was quickly followed by a whole lot of guilt.

One thing he wasn't: a poker player. He'd taken risks— on the reality show that launched his career and in business, opening restaurants. But that was different from playing a game. He didn't know if he could bluff, but this was as good a time as any to find out.

"You can talk to me, Shane." Her gaze searched his and she must have seen something. "I'm going to get coffee from the bakery and we can sit on that bench in the sun."

He saw the one she meant, a wooden bench on the side of the bakery facing Nugget Way. "There's nothing to talk about. And that will cut into your shopping time."

"The mall can wait. Somehow it will get done. This is more important."

Shane had a feeling there wouldn't be any putting her off now. "I'll get the coffee."

"No. Let me. You make sure no one takes our seats." She put a reassuring hand on his arm before disappearing inside the shop.

As soon as he sat down by himself he missed her warm presence. His darkness was no match for all that bright red hair and innate sweetness. And now he was on the spot— the classic man in conflict. He didn't want to talk about what he was dealing with because not talking was the only way to keep his secret. But obviously it was affecting him since she'd noticed his mood shifts.

He felt like a disloyal, ungrateful jerk. Gavin and Christa Roarke had done nothing but love, nurture and encourage him. He couldn't imagine a better brother or sister than Ryan and Maggie. All of them had pushed him to do what he needed to and hoped he found peace of mind. Fat chance after hearing the name Grace. It was on his birth certificate, but so what? There were probably a lot of women in and around Thunder Canyon with that name, including D. J. Traub's mother.

Gianna appeared with "to-go" cups of coffee in her hands. She sat beside him and held one out. "Cream, no sugar."

"You remembered." From breakfast just a few hours ago. Seemed like forever.

"Of course I remembered. It's my job and the boss has mentioned that I'm pretty good at it."

"He's a guy who can spot talent when he sees it."

"Also a guy who tries to hide his feelings and can't." Her expression grew sympathetic and serious. "He's got something on his mind. I'd be happy to listen and help if I can."

Shane looked up and knew why Montana was called Big Sky country. It seemed bigger, bluer and more beautiful here in Thunder Canyon. The snow-capped mountains were towering and the scenery spectacular. But that wasn't all that made this a special spot.

He'd lived all over the country in some of the biggest and most sophisticated, cosmopolitan cities. As his name recognition grew and his career soared, he'd been asked to endorse worthy causes or donate large sums of money. But he'd never been invited to cook for military families or wrap presents to brighten Christmas for a lonely soldier overseas.

That had changed here; he was a part of this community. The people had a hands-on spirit of caring that he'd never experienced before and was grateful and humbled to be part of it now. He didn't want to do anything to put him on the outside again.

And then there was Gianna. He looked at her, the sun shining on the most beautiful hair he'd ever seen. He knew she was just as beautiful inside.

"Shane?"

Damned if he did; damned if he didn't. He'd start at the beginning and wing it. "I'm adopted."

"Okay." Her expression didn't change. "The last time I checked, that wasn't a crime."

If she only knew how close that comment came to the truth.

"No, I'm aware that my story isn't one that makes a prime-time, news-magazine segment. It was too normal."

"How do you mean?" She took a sip of her coffee and angled her body toward him, listening with intense concentration.

"My parents are, quite simply, remarkable people. They're both lawyers."

"Pretty demanding careers. And yet a child was so important to them, they moved heaven and earth to have you in their lives."

"They chose me." It's what he'd always been told and a part of him had always felt special. Not anymore. "And not just me. They adopted my brother and sister—Ryan and Maggie. Also lawyers like our folks."

One of her auburn eyebrows went up. "High achievers. I realize we're not talking genes and DNA here, but how did your parents feel about your career choice?"

He smiled. "The three Roarke kids were encouraged to study what they loved and follow their passion."

"Good advice and it seems to have worked out for all of you," she commented.

"Professionally. But personally?" He shook his head.

"How do you mean? Do you have multiple wives and families stashed in cities and towns all over the country?"

"Yeah." He grinned. "Because I have so much time to pull that off. Can't you see the tabloid headline? Celebrity chef cooks up dual life."

She smiled. "So, what is it?"

"I was restless. Moved around a lot opening restaurants in Los Angeles, New York and Seattle. When I started talking about Dallas, my mother was worried."

"Why?"

"She felt I was deliberately or subconsciously avoiding settling down. And maybe I needed to look at who I was. That's when she finally gave me all the information she'd received about my birth parents from the adoption agency."

"That's incredibly courageous of her."

"No kidding." He remembered his mother's face, hesitation and concern battling it out. "She told me to use it however I wanted. Do whatever was necessary to find peace and put down roots."

"And?"

"I realized that as happy and loving as my childhood was, I'd always had questions about why I am the way I am. I wanted to connect the dots."

"What did you do?" she asked.

"Hired a private investigator."

Her eyes widened and comprehension dawned. "Is that why you took the job at The Gallatin Room here in Thunder Canyon?"

"What makes you say that?"

"You said it yourself—successful restaurants all over the country. Executive chef is a prestigious position, but this isn't Paris, New York or San Francisco. At best, it's a lateral career step. You had other reasons for taking this job."

Smart girl. He'd have to tread carefully. "Yes. The investigation and search narrowed to this town, so I contacted Grant Clifton."

"The manager of Thunder Canyon Resort."

"Right. When the previous chef's contract was up, I let Grant know I'd be interested. He jumped at the chance."

"Didn't he wonder why? A famous guy like you coming here?"

"The subject came up. I just said I'd been going at warp speed for years and wanted to throttle back for a while."

"Obviously he believed you."

"Because it was true." Shane just hadn't realized until he'd said it to Grant. And talking about it out loud now made the whole thing seem underhanded. Fruit doesn't fall far from the tree, he thought. Still, it was a good thing he'd gone about this quietly, otherwise everyone would know about his biological connection to Arthur Swinton. "But I also had personal reasons."

"To find your parents," she said. "Any luck with that since you've been here?"

He leaned forward, elbows on his knees. He didn't want her to read his expression. "Recently I found some information about my father."

"Oh, Shane—" She put her hand on his arm. "That's great. Do you know who he is?"

"Yes."

"Have you contacted him?"

"No." He laughed and heard the bitterness in the sound but hoped she didn't.

"Is he still alive?"

"Yes." And in jail. That part was best kept to himself.

"You need to talk to him."

"Not sure that's the wisest course of action."

"But it's why you started down this road in the first place." Her voice gentled when she said, "Are you worried that he'll reject you?"

That was the least of his concerns. Shane didn't want to risk *everyone else* rejecting him. The people in this town hated Arthur Swinton with the same passion that they loved being good neighbors. There was every reason to believe they would despise anyone related to their homegrown felon.

He finally met Gianna's gaze and saw the sincere desire to help shining there. She was easy to talk to, a good listener. A good friend. Maybe more than that. He didn't want to lose her by revealing what he suspected. He'd probably said too much already.

"It's complicated, Gianna."

"Of course it is. But, Shane, you're clearly not at peace the way things stand. Wouldn't it be better to get everything out in the open?"

That's what he'd thought before finding out his father was a criminal. "I'm not sure what to do with the information."

The sounds of laughter, women's and children's voices drifted to him just before he saw a large group of people round the corner. He glanced that way and the first person he recognized was D. J. Traub. They both worked at Thunder Canyon Resort restaurants so their paths crossed occasionally. They'd talked a few times.

And they both had mothers named Grace.

Gianna saw the exact moment when Shane's expression changed and he got that weird look on his face again. Before she had time to wonder what put it there, the two of them were surrounded by a big group of Traubs, Dax, D.J., their wives and three kids between them. Everyone was saying hello at once. Everyone, that is, but Shane, who stood a little apart. It was impossible to grow up in this town and not know these guys. Since she wasn't sure who Shane had met, she decided to make introductions.

"Shane Roarke, this is Dax Traub and his wife, Shandie."

"Nice to see you." Dax extended his hand.

He was a year older than his brother with dark hair and eyes, a brooding, James Dean type who oozed sex appeal.

His wife was tall, with shoulder-length blond hair cut into perfect layers.

"Dax owns a motorcycle shop here in town and Shandie works at the Clip 'n Curl," she explained.

"Nice to meet you," Shane said, cool and polite. He looked down when a little bundle of energy tripped over his shoe and nearly took a header. "Hey, buddy. You okay?"

Shandie steadied the little boy. "This is Max. Say hello to Mr. Roarke."

"Hi." The little guy had his father's dark hair and eyes. As soon as he dutifully said what was expected, he took off running down the sidewalk again.

Shandie called after him, "Slow down, Max."

Dax tugged on a young blond girl's pony tail. "This is our daughter, Kayla."

"Nice to meet you," the child said.

"The pleasure is mine, Kayla." Shane leveled all the considerable Roarke charm on her and a becoming pink stole into her cheeks.

"Sorry to be rude," a concerned Shandie said. "But I have to catch up with my son, the budding Olympic sprinter, and keep him out of trouble."

"I'll give you a hand, honey." Dax looked at Shane. "I'm sure we'll run into you again soon."

"We'll catch up with you, bro," D.J. said.

He was an inch or two shorter than his brother and not as dark. His brown hair had strands of sunlight running through it and his eyes were more chocolate than coal colored. "Shane and I have met, but I don't think you know my wife, Allaire."

The pretty, petite, blue-eyed blonde smiled. She had her hand on the shoulder of their little guy, who was quivering with the need to follow the other family and be with the kids.

"And this is our son, Alex." The proud mother smiled as she ruffled hair the same color as his father's.

"I'm four," the boy said. "Just like Max. People say I look big for four."

"I thought you were at least five and a half," Shane said seriously.

"There are days he makes me feel twice my age." D.J. shook his head.

"Mommy? Daddy? Can I go with Uncle Dax and Aunt Shandie?"

Allaire glanced up the street to the group gathered in front of a gift-shop window. "If you hurry."

"I'll run fast, like I'm already five." And he did.

"Dax?" D.J. called out and when his brother glanced over, he pointed to the boy running toward them. There was a nod of understanding and he settled a big hand on the small shoulder when Alex caught up and joined the merry little band.

Gianna glanced between them. "Is that a brother thing? Silent communication? Because my sister and I don't have that."

"Maybe because you're in different places in your lives," Allaire suggested. "Dax and D.J. both have four-year-olds and a protective streak as big as Montana."

Gianna knew it was a nice way of saying her sister Jackie was married with three kids. And she, Gianna, was a spinster with no prospects. Time to change the subject.

"So, Allaire, Lizzie was just singing your artistic praises. She said you hand-stenciled the flowers on the walls of her bakery."

"I did." The other woman smiled with pleasure.

"Beautiful job," Shane said. "I understand you're a high school art teacher."

"Yes. I wasn't cut out to be a starving artist." She looked

up at her husband. "And I'm not. Thanks to D.J.'s Rib Shack and my teaching job."

"What else do you like to work on?" Shane asked.

Gianna thought it was interesting that he was chatting up Allaire and hadn't said much to her husband. Probably the art connection. He had an interest in it judging by the collection she'd seen in his condo. The four of them moved closer to the building to let a mother with a baby in a stroller get by them on the sidewalk. The movement put Shane beside the other man.

"I really like portraits," Allaire answered. "But just for fun. I'm not very good at it. But it lets me indulge my people-watching tendency."

"She's way too modest about her amazing talent." D.J. slid an arm across her shoulders and looked at Shane. "So, how do you like Thunder Canyon?"

"Fine."

Along with the other couple, Gianna waited for him to elaborate. When he didn't, she put a teasing tone in her voice when she asked, "What happened to the poetic guy who said the scenery around here speaks to your soul?"

"If I was Shane," D.J. said with a knowing expression, "I'd never admit to that, either."

Gianna looked at Allaire and together they said, "Guy thing."

"Speaking of guys…" D.J. met her gaze, then glanced at her companion. "How's everything?"

Gianna knew he meant her love life. She'd gotten to know him since coming back to town. She'd applied for a job at the Rib Shack and he wasn't hiring, but steered her to The Gallatin Room. Then he'd taken her under his wing and become the big brother she'd always wanted.

"D.J." Allaire's voice had a scolding note to it. "Don't put her on the spot right now."

"Why?" His expression was clueless. "We talk."

"We do," she confirmed. "And I can tell you that everything is…" She'd ended up confessing to him her pathetic love life and all the time and energy she'd wasted in New York. D.J. wanted to know what was up with Shane and she wasn't going to talk about that in front of him. So she resorted to a girl's succinct fallback response. "Fine."

"You know…" Allaire glanced back and forth between the two men.

"What?" Gianna wasn't sure what was on her mind, but encouraged a change of subject.

"Speaking of people watching to indulge my artistic streak," the other woman said, "I've just noticed something."

"That I'm better looking than Ryan Reynolds?" D.J. said.

"No." She playfully punched him in the arm. "There's a very strong resemblance between you and Shane."

"Really?" Gianna studied them.

"Not the eyes." The other woman thoughtfully tapped her lip. "D.J.'s are brown and Shane's are strikingly blue. But the shape of the face is identical. And you both have a strong chin. So does Dax."

Gianna looked carefully at the two men standing side by side and saw what Allaire meant. She wondered why she'd never noticed before. Probably because she'd never seen them in the same room together, let alone side by side.

"You're right. I see it, too."

"They say everyone has a twin." D.J. pointed playfully at Shane. "Just don't pretend to be me and go changing the Rib Shack menu to snails and frog's legs."

Gianna snapped her fingers. "And you both make a living in the restaurant business. What a coincidence."

That's when she noticed Shane's weird look was back and even more intense. Not only that, he hadn't said a word since Allaire mentioned the strong resemblance. The face might resemble D.J.'s but it was not the face of the charming, playful man who'd said her fleecy pants and ratty robe were cute. Was that only last night? Seemed so much longer.

Even this morning at breakfast he'd been carefree and gallant, offering to drive her wherever she wanted to go. His mood had changed when Catherine had mentioned Presents for Patriots. Then again when Gianna had asked him about shopping for his family. That led to the revelation about him being adopted and searching for his birth parents.

He took her arm. "We should probably get to the mall."

"That's where we're going," Allaire said.

D.J. looked down at his wife. "We should meet them for lunch. You can compare the shape of Dax's face to mine and Shane's."

"I wish I could. I already have lunch plans with my mother and sister. But maybe Shane—" She'd invited him to join her but he hadn't responded one way or the other. Now Gianna felt his hand tense. Even if she were free, it was clear he'd rather eat bugs than join them.

"I can't," he said. "I have a meeting with a vendor this afternoon."

"Too bad." The other woman slid her hand into her husband's.

"How about a rain check?" D.J. suggested.

"That would be great." Gianna figured like a typical man he hadn't noticed that Shane was quiet. But she'd bet everything she had that observant Allaire had sensed something. "See you guys soon."

"You're coming to Presents for Patriots?" D.J. asked.

"Wouldn't miss it. I'm all signed up," she said, but Shane remained quiet.

"Okay, then. Bye, you two," Allaire said before they strolled down the street in the same direction the rest of the family had gone.

Shane walked her to his SUV parked in front of the bakery and handed her inside. Then he came around to the driver's side and got in. "Do you still want to go to the mall?"

His tone said he hoped to get a rain check on that, too, and suddenly she lost the Christmas spirit.

"Shane, talk to me. What's bothering you so much?"

"I already told you. Just some family stuff."

"Come on. I'm not artistic like Allaire, but I observe people, too. I'd make a lousy waitress if I didn't notice things. You barely said a word to D.J. That's not like you. You're probably one of the friendliest, most charming men I've ever met. So, I ask again. What's wrong? And don't tell me nothing."

His hand tensed on the steering wheel and a muscle in the jaw so much like D.J.'s jumped. "It's complicated."

So, back to square one. He'd shut her down again. It didn't take Cupid to clue her in that she was beating her head against the wall. By definition, romance required two people to participate in order to achieve the desired result. Clearly she was the only one here doing the work.

At least it hadn't taken her very long to figure out that he had no intention of committing. And really, it was almost funny given her history of hanging on until all hope was gone.

She'd just set a personal record in the least amount of time it took her to lose a guy.

Chapter Seven

After asking Shane to take her home, Gianna hadn't had much to say. That technically wasn't true. She'd actually had a lot to say but kept it to herself since it was impossible to have a meaningful conversation with an obviously pre-occupied man who would only tell her "it's complicated." Still, when the man said he would do something, he did it.

At Real Vintage Cowboy, Catherine Overton had her car keys. Per Shane's instructions, the car had a new battery and they'd dropped it off for her. Note to self: find out the cost and pay him back. She didn't want to owe him. On the other hand, at least she now had wheels, such as they were.

She never made it to the mall, but managed to get in a little Christmas shopping before it was time to meet her mother and sister at The Tottering Teapot. The customer base was primarily female and the restaurant was located in Old Town on Main Street near Pine, between the teenage hangout ROOTS and Mountain Bluebell Bakery. Not far from this morning's disaster with Shane.

She drove around for a while looking for a parking space because, of course, she was running late. The place did a brisk business but seemed more crowded than usual today. A lot of people were probably out Christmas shopping and stopped for lunch.

Gianna finally found a spot to park that felt like a mile up the block, then nearly jogged all the way to the entrance where the double, half-glass doors were covered with lace. She pushed her way inside and immediately the sweet scent of lighted candles surrounded her. She knew the fragrance was called Mistletoe and that made her think of kissing Shane. Thinking of him was like a sudden pinch to her heart so she tried not to.

A podium just inside the door had a sign that said "Please wait to be seated" but the hostess must have been leading another party because no one was there. Peeking into the dining room, she spotted her mother and sister already at a table.

"Because, of course, they have well-ordered lives with men who probably confide in them," she muttered to herself.

Without waiting for the hostess, she walked halfway through the restaurant. In addition to the menu of organic food, free-range chicken and grass-fed beef, everything about the place was female friendly. The tables were covered with lace tablecloths, no two the same. Food was served on thrift-store-bought, mismatched china. In deference to its name, there was an endless variety of teas, both herbal and otherwise. Normally this was Gianna's favorite restaurant, and catching up with her mother and sister was something she looked forward to. But not today.

Because getting grilled like a free-range chicken was really unappealing, Gianna pasted an everything's-just-peachy smile on her face just before sliding into the third of four chairs. The other held purses.

"Hi. Sorry I'm late. Took a while to find a place to park."

"Oh, sweetheart, don't worry about it. We haven't been here very long," her mother said.

Susan Garrison was in her early fifties and was walking, talking proof that fifty was truly the new forty. She was blond, with some chemical help at the Clip 'n Curl to cover just a sprinkling of gray. Her beautiful blue eyes had been passed on to both of her daughters.

Her sister, Jackie Blake, was about Gianna's height and had a trim figure even after three kids, but she'd inherited their mom's blond hair. There was no obvious link from either parent to Gianna's red shade and the family joke was that her father was the mailman. No one believed that since her parents only had eyes for each other.

"It seems like forever since we've done this," her sister said.

"Everyone is busy," Susan commented.

"No kidding." Gianna looked at her sister. "What's up with the kids?"

"Griffin wants to play basketball, but isn't he too short? Colin is in preschool, as you know, but he thinks he's such a big boy. Can you believe Em is two already? She's home with Frank. He doesn't have a firefighter shift for a couple of days and said I could use the break."

The brunette, twentysomething waitress brought a tray containing a china teapot filled with hot water and three cups, each with a mismatched saucer. Her name tag said "Flo." "Peppermint tea for three."

"I hope that's okay, Gianna. It's what you usually have," her mother explained.

"It's fine, Mom."

With the plastic tray under her arm, Flo pulled out her pad. "Are you ready to order?"

"I think so. I'll have the portobello mushroom sandwich and salad," Jackie said.

"Me, too." Susan folded her menu closed.

Gianna hadn't had a chance to look, but knew the choices pretty well. She usually ordered exactly like the other two but after the morning she'd had, her rebellious streak kicked in for unknown reasons.

She looked at the waitress. "Grass-fed beef burger and sweet potato fries."

"The fries are a new addition to the menu. Really yummy," Flo added. "I'll get it right out for you."

When they were alone, Susan poured hot water from the teapot into their cups. "So, how's work? What's new?"

Gianna knew the question was for her. Jackie was a stay-at-home mom and couldn't be more different from herself. She'd never had career ambitions or wanted to leave home and see the world. She married her high-school sweetheart shortly after graduation and their first child was born nine months later. Frank Blake was a county firefighter and they'd been married seven years and had two more children.

Gianna had a failed business, no romantic prospects and a junker car. She didn't really want to talk about any of it. "Work is fine."

"That's it?" Jackie asked.

"Pretty much."

"I want to hear about celebrity chef Shane Roarke." Her mother's blue eyes twinkled. "I watched *If You Can't Stand the Heat.* He's a hottie and that has nothing to do with cooking over a steaming stove."

"Mom," Gianna scolded. "What would Dad say?"

It was a deflection because she really didn't think her

carefree act would hold up to scrutiny if she was forced to talk about her boss.

"Your father would say there's nothing wrong with looking as long as I come home to him."

"Frank would agree with that." Her sister looked thoughtful. "This isn't the first time I've noticed that he and Dad are a lot alike."

Susan took a cautious sip of the hot tea, then set the cup on the saucer. "They're both good men. Solid. Stable. Dependable. It's what eased my worries a little bit when you insisted on getting married so young."

"It all worked out for the best," Jackie said.

And then some. It was everything Gianna wanted. Up until this morning she'd been sure Shane was cut from the same cloth as the other two men, but now she didn't know what to think. His behavior had changed so suddenly. Where he was concerned, her emotions were all over the map. One minute she was angry, the next worried about whatever was so "complicated."

"Are you okay, honey?"

"Hmm?" Gianna had zoned out and it took a couple of seconds to realize her mother was speaking to her. "Sorry, Mom. I'm fine. Just tired."

"Any particular reason?"

"No. Just that time of the year when we're all busy."

It wouldn't do any good to tell them that she'd lost sleep because of playing in the snow last night with Shane, then he drove her home and made love to her. Her head was still spinning from the speed at which everything had changed.

She looked at her sister. "What's going on with you?"

"Things are good. The kids aren't sick and I hope we make it through the holidays with everyone healthy." She crossed her fingers for luck. "Griffin is in the Christmas pageant at his school. Colin's preschool is going to the hospital to sing carols for the patients. I'm the room mother in both of their classes and responsible for the holiday parties. I love doing it, but when Emily is old enough for school, I'm not sure how I can spread myself that thin."

"You need minions." Gianna remembered talking about that with Shane and wondered how long casual conversation would set off reminders of him.

"She has minions," Susan said. "It's called family."

Jackie snapped her fingers. "That reminds me."

"What?" Gianna and her mother said at the same time.

Her sister grabbed her purse from the chair and pulled something from the side pocket. It was an oblong-shaped piece of cardstock and she handed one to each of them. "This is the Blake family Christmas card."

Gianna's heart pinched again in a different way as she looked at her sister's beautiful family. Handsome dark-haired Frank with four-year-old Colin on his lap. Beautiful Jackie holding Emily. She was wearing a sweet little red-velvet dress, white leggings and black-patent shoes. Griffin, seven and a half, stood just behind his parents, little arms trying to reach around their shoulders.

"Oh, sis—" Gianna's voice caught. "This is a fantastic picture."

"It really is, honey." Susan smiled fondly.

"Thanks." Her sister beamed. "It's a Christmas miracle. You have no idea the level of difficulty there is in getting a decent photo of three kids and two adults. No one is crying and by that I mean Frank and I. There are no spots on the clothes—at least none that show up."

Gianna laughed in spite of the fact that she was simultaneously rocking a case of jealousy and feelings of failure. She loved her sister very much and was so happy for her. But the picture she held in her hands was everything she'd ever wanted and thought by now she would have. She was thirty years old and had nothing to show for it except a string of broken dreams and long, unsuccessful relationships.

She wasn't sure Shane could be considered a relationship, but he was definitely the shortest. So it didn't make sense that what happened with him hurt so much more than all the others.

And it was going to get worse. She had to see him at work in a couple of hours.

Shane paced back and forth in the living room of his condo but today the fantastic mountain view and heavenly blue sky did nothing to fill up his soul. On the other hand, his mind was overflowing, mostly about how rude he'd been to Gianna that morning.

"I'm an idiot." An idiot who was talking to himself. "At the very least she just thinks I'm nuts. It's complicated? How does that explain anything?"

His cell phone rang and he plucked it from the case on his belt then checked the caller ID because he didn't want to talk to anyone unless absolutely necessary. This person was most definitely necessary.

He smiled and hit the talk button. "Hi, Mom."

"Shane. Is it really you? Not your voice mail?"

"Okay. I officially feel guilty."

She laughed. "Is this a bad time? Are you working? I don't want to interrupt—"

"You're not interrupting anything." Except him beating himself up. He had a little time before work. And facing Gianna. "I'm at home."

"Great." Christa Roarke's voice suited her. She was strong, sweet, tough and tender. A green-eyed brunette whose face showed the traumas and triumphs of life but remained beautiful. She practiced family law and after struggling to have a family of her own, it seemed appropriate.

"Is Dad okay?" Gavin Roarke was the strongest man he knew, but Shane always needed to check.

"Fine. Why?"

"Ryan and Maggie?" His siblings, lawyers like their parents. He'd wondered more than once if that's part of what made him question who he was. Though they were all adopted, he was the only one who didn't follow in their parents' footsteps, but took a completely different career path. He couldn't remember when he'd seriously begun to wonder why.

"Your brother and sister are fine." There was humor in her voice. "But the focus of your questions leads me to believe you think I called because of a family crisis."

"Did you?"

"Everyone here in L.A. is fine."

"Good." That left him the only family member in a mess. "What can I do for you, Mom?"

"I just haven't talked to you for a while." There was a slight hesitation before she added, "That comment was in no way meant to make you feel guilty."

He laughed. "If you say so."

"Maybe because it's the holidays and you're so far away, I've just been thinking a lot about you. Wondering how you are."

He stood beside the floor-to-ceiling windows and leaned a shoulder against the wall as he looked out. His mother was as transparent as the glass. She knew why he'd come to Thunder Canyon and was fishing for information. "I'm okay."

There was silence on the other end of the line for a few moments before she asked, "That's it? Just okay?"

"Yeah."

"This is why you're not an attorney like the rest of the

Roarkes. Practicing law frequently requires the use of words and apparently that's not your strength."

He grinned. "I communicate through food."

"That's all well and good. The culinary world loves you. The camera loves you. And I love you. But it's a mother's job to encourage her child to use words."

"It's a dirty job, I guess, but someone has to do it."

"And you know what an overachiever I can be," she said.

"What is it you're asking, Mom?"

"You just love to torture me, don't you?" She sighed. "Okay. You asked for it. Here comes the maternal cross-examination."

"I can hardly wait." A rustling sound on the line made him picture her sitting up straight in the chair, probably behind the desk in her office.

"Mr. Roarke, you've lived in Thunder Canyon, Montana, for nearly six months now. How is it going?"

He thought about the question and knew she was asking how the search for his birth parents was progressing. When he'd first stepped foot in the town something clicked into place inside him and it seemed crazy at the time. But the more he learned, the longer he stayed, the less crazy that feeling felt. Still, he wasn't ready to tell his family what was going on. So much of it was conjecture. Getting into her milieu, he only had half the facts to build a case.

So, Shane decided to use his words to go in a different direction. "When I made the decision to come here, I braced myself for a wilderness adventure."

"Survivor Montana?" she teased.

"Something like that." He studied the jagged snow-capped peaks with evergreen trees standing out in stark relief against the whiteness. "You can research anything on the internet, but there's no way to experience a place until you do it in person."

"There's a reverence in your voice, as if you're in church."

"Someone else said the same thing to me," he answered, thinking of Gianna. "And it feels like being in the presence of God sometimes. You can't know unless you see."

"And what do you know now, Shane?"

"I like this place. More than I thought." He pretended she wasn't asking about his search. "Thunder Canyon is small. Really small compared to anywhere I've ever lived."

"That could be a double-edged sword."

"People talk." He knew that and what he'd uncovered could give them a lot to talk about. "Around here everyone knows your business even if you haven't shared it with them. But that can also be a good thing. When there's a problem, they don't look the other way. They don't avoid getting involved or feel inconvenienced. Folks help each other out."

"And you like that?"

"Let me put it this way," he said. "I've donated money to charity and felt good about it, but was never personally touched by the cause. But it's different here. There's no comparison, no way to describe how good it feels to use your talent to make a difference. To be included in a cause bigger than yourself."

"Such as?"

"Just before Thanksgiving I prepared a dinner for the families of military members serving overseas. You could see the gratitude in their eyes, Mom. It was a fantastic feeling."

"Sounds wonderful."

"Of course I didn't do it alone. The staff at The Gallatin Room pitched in. Gianna was pretty amazing."

"Gianna?"

"Gianna Garrison. She's one of the waitresses who volunteered her time to serve that dinner." He pictured the sassy redhead with the beautiful smile that warmed him in dark places he hadn't even been aware of. "She worked her tail off and I never once saw her anything but considerate. Always laughing."

"Is she pretty?"

"What does that have to do with anything?"

"Humor me." There was a tone that said resistance was futile.

"She's very attractive." Such plain words to describe someone so bright, so special. And before his mother asked, he added, "A blue-eyed redhead."

"Hmm."

He wished he could see her expression. "What does that mean?"

"Nothing. Go on."

"That's it. I was finished."

"Hardly." Along with sweet and strong, his mother's voice could also be sarcastic. "There's a lot more you're not saying."

Mental note, he thought. Never play poker with this woman. But he added something that was completely true and also too simple to explain what he felt. "I like her."

"That does it. I really want to meet the new woman in your life."

"That's not how it is." At least not after the way he'd acted this morning. He probably blew it big time.

He just hadn't been able to pull off a casual act after Catherine Overton mentioned D.J.'s mother's name was Grace. If their mothers sharing a first name was the only coincidence, he could have laughed it off. But then Allaire Traub commented on his resemblance to Dax and D.J. She'd stopped short of calling it a family resemblance, but...

He and D.J. both had the food-service industry in common and every time he'd seen the other man there'd been a feeling. A shared sense of humor. A connection that Shane couldn't explain. Because they were brothers?

It *was* complicated. If he'd told Gianna all of his suspicions, she'd think he was crazy and call the shrink squad. Shane had heard the rumors of Swinton's unrequited love for Grace Traub, but everyone laughed it off as the raving of a lunatic. What if that was true? What if Arthur Swinton had slept with Dax and D.J.'s mother and he, Shane, was the result?

"Shane?"

His mother's voice yanked him out of the dark turn his thoughts had taken. "Sorry. What did you say?"

"I asked how it is with you and Gianna?"

It was nowhere because he'd pushed her away. Even a bad shrink would say it was because he didn't want to see the look of disgust in her eyes when she learned who his father was. Why would she not believe that an evil man's son didn't have evil in his DNA?

"I consider her a friend," he finally said.

"Hostile witness."

"Really, Mom?" He had to smile. "Now you're going all lawyer on me?"

"That's what you do when a witness holds back." She sighed. "But, it's all right. You're entitled to your secrets."

That word grated on him. He was learning the hard way that secrets could corrode the soul. Should he come clean with Gianna, give her the explanation? Maybe stop the blackness inside him from spreading? The risk was that everyone in town would find out. But maybe if he asked her to keep it to herself, it might be possible to control the flow of information even in a small town.

When he didn't comment, his mother continued, "Another reason I called is…what are your plans for Christmas?"

"I hadn't really thought that far ahead." What with everything else on his mind.

"It's a couple of weeks, so not really that far ahead. Will we see you for the holidays?" Her voice was carefully casual, an indication that seeing him meant a lot.

The truth was he missed his family. He'd never not been there for Christmas. No matter where he worked his heart was with the Roarkes—his parents and his siblings. Nothing he found out would ever change that.

"Of course I'll be there."

"Wonderful." There was a subtle sound of relief in her voice. "We'll look forward to seeing you, sweetheart."

"Same here, Mom."

"Hold on." There were muffled voices in the background, then she came back on the line. "I'm sorry, Shane. My next appointment is here."

"No problem, Mom. I have to get to work."

"Love you, son."

"Love you, too."

He clicked off and thought about the conversation. It didn't escape his notice that he no longer thought of Los Angeles as home. Something twisted in his chest when he opened the French door and walked out on the balcony to look at the big sky and mountains. The cold snapped through him and sliced inside.

He wasn't at all sure he would survive Montana unscathed. This place had become home and Gianna had become more important than he'd intended. It was entirely possible that he could be more lost now than when he'd first arrived in Thunder Canyon.

Chapter Eight

At work Gianna looked over the empty dining room, searching for anything out of place. Silverware was wrapped in cloth napkins and ready in a corner, out of the view of customers. Fresh linens and flower vases were on the tables along with lighted candles. She'd done everything ahead of time that could possibly be done and not compromise the quality and freshness of food.

The service business was always a delicate balance, not unlike navigating a relationship. Never give anyone a reason not to come back, but if a mistake was made, do whatever was necessary to make things right.

With all the prep work done, this would be a good time to grab a quick bite to eat. At lunch with her mother and sister she'd lost her appetite, but was starving now. The rest of the staff had already finished their pre-service meal and were gearing up for a busy night. A local company was having their Christmas party in the banquet room.

In the kitchen there was food left from the staff meal. She was just taking a bite when Shane walked in. This was the first time she'd seen him alone since he'd dropped her off at her apartment this morning. Not that she'd done anything wrong, or that she wanted to give him a reason to come back, but speaking of making things right... They did have to work together, at least for the time being.

There was a nanosecond of awkwardness between them before she finally said, "Hi. How are you?"

"Keeping my head above water." He shrugged. "How's the car?"

"Not getting any younger and still holding together with bubble gum and prayer." That produced a smile, which was good to see. "But running now, thanks to you. I left a check for the battery on the desk in your office."

"You didn't have to. I was happy to take care of it. And I'll be tearing up that check." She opened her mouth to protest, but he held up his hand. "No argument. Just say thank you."

"All right. Thank you. I appreciate it very much."

"You're welcome." He hesitated a moment. "So you saw your mother and sister?"

"Yes."

He moved closer, leaned a hip against the counter beside her and crossed his arms over his chest. The spicy scent of his cologne burrowed inside her and pushed every nerve into a spasm of need. If she hadn't been with him skin to skin maybe she could fight off this overwhelming feeling, but that wasn't the case. She had slept with him and there was no way to unremember the practically perfect way his body had felt against hers.

"How was lunch?" His gaze settled on hers.

Why was he suddenly so chatty? She'd take it as a good thing if the shadows weren't still in his eyes, just the way he'd looked outside of Mountain Bluebell Bakery. But her questions, even though asked with the intention of helping, hadn't helped either one of them.

She ran a finger around the edge of her plate. "It's always good to catch up with Jackie and my mom. They're busy getting ready for Christmas. Making plans."

"Apparently this is the day for it." He rubbed a hand across the back of his neck.

"Oh?" She took a bite of her food, although her appetite was missing in action again.

"My mother called."

"How was it?" He'd already opened that door by asking her the same question.

"Before or after she let me know I don't phone home often enough?"

"I can see how that would lead directly into holiday plans," she agreed.

"It did. And I'm going to Los Angeles."

"You're leaving?"

"For Christmas," he confirmed.

Even she had heard the shock and hurt in her voice. If only she were a computer and could backspace and delete those two words. She had no claim on him. Yes, he'd taken her to bed and she'd gone enthusiastically. But there was no reason to think it was more than fun. They'd gone into it with the understanding that one or both of them would be leaving town. Nothing serious.

Except somewhere in her subconscious she must have been thinking about spending the holiday with him. Otherwise she wouldn't feel like the rug had been yanked out from under her because he wouldn't be here for Christmas. The depth of her disappointment was a surprise, a very unwelcome one.

"Gianna—" He cupped her cheek in his palm. "Please don't look like that."

Obviously she wasn't very successfully hiding her disappointment. "I'm not looking any way. Not on purpose. You just surprised me. It's your first Christmas in Thunder Canyon and the way you talked—" She'd assumed when a place filled up your soul, it's where you'd want to be at the most wonderful time of the year. Apparently his soul was taken and this was proof that she had no claim on his heart. "I understand. They're your family."

"They are. And I love them." His gaze searched hers and he let out a long breath. "Look, I feel like a jerk—"

"No. Please don't. Of course you should be with your family. I didn't mean anything. I'm fine."

"You are fine." For just an instant as he caressed her cheek with his thumb, heat burned in his eyes. Then it was gone and the shadows returned. "And I acted like an idiot earlier. You deserve an explanation."

"That's not necessary—"

"I know it's not, but I want to tell you. I need to talk about this with someone. It's eating me up inside." There was a dark and dangerous expression on his face. He took her hand and led her away from the noise and bustle of the kitchen, into the pantry where he'd kissed her. He didn't look like he planned to kiss her now.

So she was right to be concerned about him. "What is it, Shane? Of course you can talk to me. I'm happy to listen."

"You might change your mind when I tell you what's going on."

"Be a Band-Aid."

"What?"

"Do it quick. Just spit it out."

He hesitated for a moment, then said, "Arthur Swinton is my biological father."

Gianna couldn't believe she'd heard him correctly. "What?"

"The man who embezzled from the city, disappeared with the money and was behind all the bad stuff that happened to the Traub family is my father."

"You're joking."

"If I was going to joke, it wouldn't be about that." He dragged his fingers through his hair. "The way everyone in town feels about that weasel makes him the last man on the planet I'd claim for a father unless it was true."

She stared at him. "Are you sure about this?"

"I have a DNA test confirming it to a ninety-nine percent certainty."

Her brain was spinning. "But don't you need a sample from him? I thought he was in jail."

"He is." Shane's gaze slid away for a moment. "I told you my mother gave me all the information she had on my birth parents? She also told me the adoption records were sealed and she didn't know what good it would do."

"Right."

"The private investigator said with everything on computers, now no records can be completely sealed. Nothing is hack-proof. My biological mother's first name and the first initial of her last name are on the birth certificate. It only has my father's initials. The guy I hired found the hospital and narrowed the search to Thunder Canyon. After tightening the parameters of age, names with those initials, then cross-referencing employment and personal interests, which included political ambitions, one name stood out."

"Arthur Swinton was on the town council for years," she remembered.

"He ran for mayor against Bo Clifton on a family-values platform." Bitterness hardened his eyes. "How hypocriti-

Send For
2 FREE BOOKS
Today!

I accept your offer!

Please send me two free
Harlequin® Special Edition
novels and two mystery gifts
(gifts worth about $10).
I understand that these books
are completely free — even
the shipping and handling will
be paid—and I am under no
obligation to purchase anything, ever,
as explained on the back of this card.

235/335 HDL FNPH

Please Print

FIRST NAME

LAST NAME

ADDRESS

APT.#   CITY

STATE/PROV.   ZIP/POSTAL CODE

Visit us online at
www.ReaderService.com

NO POSTAGE
NECESSARY
IF MAILED
IN THE
UNITED STATES

BUSINESS REPLY MAIL
FIRST-CLASS MAIL   PERMIT NO. 717   BUFFALO, NY

POSTAGE WILL BE PAID BY ADDRESSEE

THE READER SERVICE
PO BOX 1867
BUFFALO NY 14240-9952

cal is that? Add being a fraud of a human being to his long list of sins."

Gianna was in shock. "I was in New York when that happened, but my mom told me what was going on. How did you get the DNA?"

"The P.I. visited him in jail. He made up something about being a journalist and doing a story on Thunder Canyon politicians. Swinton was only too happy to talk about how he was a victim of the Traubs. That they always hated him."

"And the investigator was able to get something to compare DNA?"

Shane nodded. "A soda can. He said it was easy and the guy never suspected anything."

"And the test is back?"

"I got a report just before Thanksgiving." His mouth twisted as if he'd eaten something bad. "*There's* something to be thankful for. Being the son of Thunder Canyon's most despised person."

"Oh, Shane—" Gianna suddenly got it. He was concerned that if anyone found out about this the whole town would turn against him, making him an outcast in the place he'd come to love. And the worst part was that he could be right. Some great person she was to talk to. She couldn't think of anything helpful to say.

"It will be okay." That was lame. So she put her hand on his arm.

"Careful." He pulled away from her touch. "You probably don't want to get too close to me."

"Don't be ridiculous. This doesn't change the good man you are." She met his gaze even as the struggle to wrap her mind around this raged inside her. "Did the investigator find out about your mother?"

"No." He slid his fingers into the pockets of his jeans. "But you've heard the rumors of Grace Traub and Arthur

Swinton. How he ranted and raved about them being a couple. Everyone in town thought he was just a wacko, but the name on my birth certificate is Grace S. Dax and D.J.'s mother's name was Grace."

"That doesn't prove anything."

"Not by itself. But you heard Allaire Traub. The resemblance—"

"Shane—" The ramifications of that rippled through her. "Do you think you're related to the Traubs?"

"I don't know. But that family has every reason to hate the man. He tried to destroy them, personally and professionally. How do you think they'd feel to find out he's my father and we could be half brothers? What does that information do to their mother's memory?"

He was so right. This *was* complicated and that word didn't even do it justice.

"Gianna?"

She looked up as the blond, thirtyish restaurant hostess poked her head in the door. "Hi, Ashley. What's up?"

"I just seated a party of four in your station."

"Thanks. I'll be right there." She looked at Shane. "I don't want to leave you like this—"

"It's okay." But there was nothing okay in the look on his face, or the tension coiled in his body. "We have a job to do."

She nodded, then slid off the stool and tossed her food in the trash. If only her thoughts could go with it. The fact was she needed time alone to let all this sink in. She wasn't sure how she felt, which was why Shane was justified in his concern. If this information got out, his reputation and standing in Thunder Canyon could be destroyed.

Shane wasn't sure if this was the smartest move, but he'd felt compelled to drop by D.J.'s Rib Shack. Both of their restaurants were on resort grounds and when business slowed at The Gallatin Room, he'd left the sous-chef in charge, with orders to call if there was an emergency.

It was possible he was jumping to conclusions about Grace Traub and Arthur Swinton. Somehow he couldn't think of the man as his dad. And he couldn't very well ask D.J. about what happened, so he wasn't sure what this visit would accomplish. Curiosity, maybe.

Now he stood in the doorway of the Rib Shack looking around. Really looking. He'd been in here before, but it all felt different now, given the things he'd learned. There were a few customers scattered around the large, open dining room in this primarily family restaurant. Booths lined the exterior with picnic-style tables and benches filling the center. The walls were covered with sepia-toned pictures of cowboys, ranches and a hand-painted mural depicting the town's history. He was surprised it didn't include a section with Arthur Swinton being led away in handcuffs.

That kind of thinking proved that this was a stupid idea. He started to leave then spotted D. J. Traub himself walking toward him. So much for a clean getaway.

"Shane. Hi." The other man held out his hand and gave him a firm handshake. "To what do I owe the pleasure of a visit from Thunder Canyon's celebrity chef?"

"Celebrity?" He shrugged. "I had an opportunity. I'm just a guy who's fearless with food."

"You just happened to be fearless on reality TV in front of millions of women. Thunder Canyon ladies are lucky to have you."

Shane couldn't suppress a grin at the good-natured teasing. "It's a dirty job, but someone has to do it and do it well."

"Modest, too. I can respect that." D.J.'s dark eyes glittered with amusement. "Do you have time for a beer?"

"Why not?" Actually he could think of a lot of reasons, but his curiosity was telling him to follow through on this.

"Follow me."

The other man led him to a quiet corner in the back of the restaurant where there was a table and two wooden barrel-backed chairs. He said something to one of the waitresses and she returned with a couple of frosty mugs of beer.

"Thanks, Jan," D.J. said to her. He looked across the small table at Shane. "So, how are things at The Gallatin Room?"

"Busy. Business is up compared to last year."

"That could have something to do with the famous and fearless chef running the place."

"Whatever." Shane took a sip of his beer. "It's all good."

He couldn't say the same for his personal life. Probably he didn't deserve it, but at least Gianna was speaking to him. If only he could forget the look in her eyes when he'd confessed about who his father was. He wouldn't have blamed her if she'd run screaming from the room.

"What about you?" he asked, glancing around. "How are things here?"

"The books look better than they have in a while. Grant Clifton says resort traffic is better than it's been in a while, so there's a direct connection. Part of the increase could be because Traub Oil Montana is gearing up, bringing jobs into the area."

"That means more families," Shane commented.

"Right. Since that's the Rib Shack demographic, we've been more in demand. I've been able to hire some people. Business is improving."

"Do you like it? Food service?"

D.J. nodded. "Yeah. I enjoy the chaos, seeing the customers having fun. How about you?"

"Can't imagine doing anything else. The complexity, creativity and everything you just said, too."

Their careers were in the same field and it felt good to

talk to someone who understood. They each filled a different niche under the Thunder Canyon Resort umbrella. Not for the first time he wondered if it was a coincidence or something in the genes.

Their thoughts must have been traveling a parallel path because D.J. said, "I'm glad our customer base is different."

"You mean because I get to serve romantic dinners to local lovers Forrest Traub and Angie Anderson? And budding couples like Ben Walters and Kay Bausch?"

"Ben and Kay?" One of D.J.'s dark eyebrows lifted in surprise.

"I understand it was a blind date." And now he was talking about people as if he was just like everyone else here in Thunder Canyon.

Gianna had told him about the older couple. She thought it was cute and he agreed. He also thought Gianna was pretty cute and so much more. He wasn't sure how he'd have come this far without her. She'd listened to him and he felt better after confiding in her. Although not if his revelation had cost him that connection with her. But that was something for later.

"Apparently Austin Anderson set up the two of them."

D.J. looked amused. "So you're saying your place is all about romance?"

"And you get what comes after. Families." Shane had meant it in a teasing way, but had an uncomfortable hollow feeling inside, a sense of loneliness he'd never felt before. That something was missing from his own life. "You're a lucky man, D.J. To have Allaire and your son."

"I've loved her for a long time." The other man toyed with his mug. "You know she was married to my brother Dax for a while."

"No, I didn't." Shane was surprised. The two brothers had looked like they were extraordinarily close and he'd envied the shared bond of growing up together. How could they maintain that when they had both loved the same woman?

"The look on your face says you've got a lot of questions about how we can still hang out." D.J. smiled. "It was a long time ago. They both knew it wasn't right and stayed friends. Things have a way of working out the way they're supposed to."

Shane wasn't so sure about that but hoped it proved true. He felt comfortable with this guy. Liked him. D.J. was honest, funny and could maintain a relationship with his brother, even though they'd been married to the same woman. That was extraordinarily open-minded. Maybe a friendship was possible, even if the truth of Shane's real father came out.

But it wasn't coming out now. He traced a finger through the condensation on the outside of his mug.

"So, do you think the Packers will make it to the Super Bowl?" D.J. must have sensed the need for a subject change.

"Not if the Forty-Niners have anything to say about it."

"Ah, a California guy loyal to the state's teams."

Shane shrugged. "I've moved around a lot. Seattle for a while. New York. Los Angeles is just where I grew up."

"But you could be persuaded to root for the Packers?"

"Maybe." He looked around the big room. "Is this where you hold the Presents for Patriots event?"

The other man nodded. "We've been collecting donations for a while now. Storing them in a back room here. Small electronics, toiletries, socks, candy. Baked goods are brought in the day when all the volunteers wrap and box it all up for shipping out."

"It's quite an undertaking."

"I'm privileged to do it. Family is precious," D.J. said,

suddenly serious and sincere. "No one knows that better than I do."

"Me, too." Catherine had mentioned that his mother died when he was young and there was a time that connecting with his dad was difficult. Shane loved his parents and would do anything for them, but he had different family issues.

"Our military men and women sacrifice so much every day," D.J. continued. "But even more this time of year. They give up holidays with their loved ones so that we can be safe and secure and enjoy ours. In some small way what we do says thanks for that."

Shane could see for himself that the other man felt deeply about family and roots. Would he understand why Shane needed to find out about his birth parents? Would D.J. have done the same thing if he'd been given up for adoption?

D.J. took a swallow of beer. "Wow, I can't believe it's been a year already."

"Since the last Presents for Patriots?"

"That. The holidays. Rose and Austin were married last year on Christmas Day." D.J. looked thoughtful. "It was a year ago that she was kidnapped."

"What?" Shane couldn't believe he'd heard right. Things like that didn't happen in Thunder Canyon.

"That's right. You weren't here then."

"She was kidnapped? By who?"

"Jasper Fowler."

The man who was linked to Arthur Swinton. It seemed as if everything bad that happened in this town could be traced back to his father. "What happened?"

"Rose works in public relations for the mayor and was helping clean out paperwork from the previous administration. She found evidence of Swinton's embezzling money from the city council and a link to Fowler as an accomplice."

Shane's stomach knotted. "I heard about that."

"Common knowledge," D.J. agreed. "But everyone thought Swinton had died in jail. Turned out he faked a heart attack and with inside help he escaped. He and Fowler conspired to ruin my business and launder the stolen money through The Tattered Saddle."

"Which is now Real Vintage Cowboy." Shane was concentrating on not reacting as if any of this concerned him personally.

"Right. Rose decided to pay Fowler a visit and ask him about what she found. It never occurred to her that the man could be dangerous. But she was wrong. He was desperate and crazy and took her at gunpoint."

"But she got away." That was stating the obvious but he couldn't manage much more than that.

"Smart girl." There was a dark satisfaction in D.J.'s eyes. "She managed to call Austin and leave the cell line open while she talked to the old man about where he was taking her. They were intercepted by her brother Jackson and Austin. I think a couple more of her brothers showed up, too, and then the cops. Fowler gave up Swinton and he was re-arrested. He won't be getting out of jail anytime soon."

"That's quite a story."

D.J. shook his head. "It really ticks me off that the rumor linking my mother to Swinton refuses to go away."

"I can understand that." If Shane could make his own connection to the man go away he'd do it in a nanosecond.

"Swinton is corrupt. A convicted criminal."

Anger and resentment twisted together in D.J.'s expression along with distaste and revulsion. Shane hoped it wasn't a preview of what he could expect. If he had it to do over again, he'd refuse to take the information his mother gave him. It came under the heading of be careful what you wish for. Or let sleeping dogs lie. When you went out of your way to connect the dots, you might not like the picture that emerged.

"I can't believe people would think my mother could be involved with someone like that," D.J. continued. "No way Grace Traub would associate with him. Actually it would have been before she married my dad. She'd have been Grace Smith then. She'd never have gone out with Swinton."

Shane went cold inside as the dots connected. If she'd only gone out with him, Shane thought, he and D.J. wouldn't be sitting here talking. Under the table his hands curled into fists. All the puzzle pieces fell into place and explained his resemblance to the other man. Only a DNA test would prove it to a ninety-nine percent certainty, but Grace S. was his mother's name. Smith was such a common last name that the P.I. wouldn't be able to pin down his mother's identity for certain. Evidence from his own search was piling up, though.

Shane was convinced that Dax and D. J. Traub were his half brothers.

Chapter Nine

Gianna stood in the shadows off to the side in The Gallatin Room. The customers at her tables were enjoying various courses of their meals. At the moment there was nothing for her to do and it was nice to take a breather. Interrupting every five seconds to ask if they needed anything was as bad as ignoring them.

Especially when there was romance in this room. Candles still flickered on pristine white tablecloths and there was a quiet hum of conversation and laughter. *She* didn't feel much like laughing as she watched Shane performing the public relations part of his job.

The information about who his father was had overshadowed her disappointment that he wouldn't be here for Christmas. What he'd talked to her about a little while ago was shocking enough, and then he'd disappeared. He was back now looking even more troubled.

He frequently schmoozed with the customers, moving

from table to table, meeting and greeting, using his natural charm and enjoying the connection. He was doing that now, but something was off. There was tension on his face in spite of the smile, and something like shock in his eyes. Each encounter was brief and smacked of duty, not the usual friendly and relaxed way he interacted. The lines of his body looked tight, as if he might snap.

Bonnie moved beside her and let out a long breath. "It's been so busy. I haven't had a chance to talk."

"Tell me about it." She smiled at her friend, then glanced at Shane. "How's everything with you?"

"Jim and I broke up."

"Bon—" Gianna gave her a quick hug. "I'm sorry. What happened?"

"He wasn't that into me." She tried to look spunky, but the disappointment leaked through. "I'm swearing off men. It's time to go back to college. No distractions."

"College is good. But don't back yourself into a corner with grand declarations about no relationships." If anyone could sympathize it was Gianna. "You really thought he was the one."

"Isn't it a rule or a law of physics or something that you can't be in love by yourself?"

"It's definitely more fun with two."

Her friend's gaze wandered to their boss, who was on his way back to the kitchen. "What's with Shane tonight?"

Gianna had to decide how to answer that question. She'd seen romances here at work burn bright and hot then fizzle and get awkward. The ones involved always thought they were discreet and keeping things under the radar. But when people worked as closely together as they did in food service, secrets were hard to keep. Although she'd managed. She hadn't said anything about sleeping with the boss, and wondered if her friend had noticed a change in anything.

"You think he's different tonight?"

"Not at the start of my shift," Bonnie said carefully.

"Then when?"

"The last hour or so. I've put in requests from customers, nothing out of the ordinary because he insists on one hundred percent satisfaction. But he's had to redo several meals, like his mind is on something else. One guy asked for no mango, not even a garnish on the plate. Shane put on the mango. Fortunately I noticed and fixed it."

"That's so unlike him," Gianna said.

"Tell me about it. His mind is somewhere else and the rest of him is on autopilot. I had to tell him about the mistake. He's always encouraged us to do that. It's one of the things I like best, that he's not a prima donna. But this time he practically bit my head off. He was gone for a while and came back different."

Gianna had noticed that, too. "Do you know where he went?"

"No. He's not in the habit of confiding in me."

Gianna couldn't say the same, except about where he'd gone, but when he walked back in the kitchen, he looked like a shell-shocked soldier on the battlefield.

"Don't be too hard on him." She looked at her petite, brown-eyed friend. "He's going through some stuff."

"So am I. Isn't everyone?" Bonnie dragged her fingers through her pixie haircut. "But it's not okay to bring it to work."

"We need to cut him some slack. He's dealing with more than a broken relationship."

Her friend's eyes widened into an "aha" expression. "Is there something you'd like to tell me?"

"Such as?"

"For starters how do you know so much about him? Like

what could he be dealing with other than cooking a filet to the customer's exact specifications?"

"Oh, you know—"

How could she? Who could possibly guess that he was Arthur Swinton's son?

And Gianna was torn. Part of her really wanted to talk to someone about her conflicted feelings and Bonnie was her best friend. But this information had the potential to ruin Shane's life.

"No, I don't know." Bonnie stared at her, waiting. "What's going on with you and Shane?"

"That's a good question." Maybe she could share just a little. "Remember when you called in sick?"

"Right, the Swiss travel delegation was here."

"I told you he invited me to his place and cooked dinner to thank me for efficiently filling in."

"More like working your butt off." Interest sparkled in her friend's eyes. "Yeah, I remember you thought it got awkward at the end."

"It did until…"

Did she say that out loud?

Bonnie's raised eyebrow told her she had. "Until he saved his moves for the pantry?"

Gianna's cheeks burned and she was grateful for the romantic lighting that hid her reaction. "You saw?"

"You didn't just ask me that. Of course I saw. Not much goes on in a restaurant kitchen that doesn't get seen by someone." There was nothing but teasing and the concern of a friend in her tone. "So give. I want details."

Gianna sighed. "It was maybe the best kiss of my entire life."

"In the pantry? He couldn't have picked somewhere—I don't know—with ambience?"

"That's what I said. He promised to make it up to me

because the first kiss didn't happen on the balcony of his condo."

"He passed up moonlight and a view of the mountains for a closet at work?" Bonnie sounded shocked and appalled. "That's just wrong in so many ways."

"He made up for it."

"Did he now?"

"It's not what you think," Gianna protested.

"I think you slept with him."

"Okay. It is what you think, but— But we're just having fun. No expectations."

"No one expects to fall in love. It just happens." Sadness slid back into her friend's eyes.

"It's not going to happen to me. Been there, done that. Not again." But caring about him was different, wasn't it? She hoped so because she couldn't help caring.

"Look, I know you, G. You don't have to pretend with me. You're not the type to take advantage of a situation. You pull your own weight and work harder than anyone because it's who you are." Her smile was sincere. "But if he hurts you, I'll make him sorry even if it costs me my job."

"Thanks, Bon." Gianna meant that from the bottom of her heart.

Her friend glanced at her tables. "I have to clear salads. Then hope the real Shane is back in control."

"Thanks for listening."

"Anytime."

"And Bonnie?"

"Right." She grinned. "I'll keep it to myself."

Gianna wasn't sure whether or not she felt better. And right now it didn't matter. She was here to work. Her shift was nearly over; the hostess wasn't seating any more customers. It was time to take care of her last few tables for the evening.

Gianna checked in with the diners and brought whatever was needed. With a little time on her hands, she walked back in the kitchen. Shane was the only one there, standing with his back against the stainless-steel counter, his dark eyebrows drawn together. This was not a man thinking happy thoughts.

"Shane?"

He looked up. "Hmm?"

"What's wrong?" She held up a hand when he opened his mouth, body language signaling a denial. "Don't waste your breath. It's obvious something is bothering you. I'm not the only one who noticed."

"I don't want to talk about it."

"Where did you go before?" she asked, trying to draw him out.

"What part of 'I don't want to talk about it' did you not understand?"

She blinked up at him. "Okay. It's just that you look upset. I wanted to help."

He drew in a deep breath. "Sorry. I didn't mean to snap. It's just—I can't do this now."

He stared at her long and hard before he simply turned and walked out the back door of the restaurant. Gianna started to go after him then stopped. She had to finish up her shift, but she hated the delay. Her heart ached for him because he had the look of a man who desperately needed to get something off his chest.

What more could there be? He'd already confessed who his father was. The disclosure had really rocked her and at the time, she wasn't sure how she felt. But she did now. Her feelings about him hadn't changed. He was a good man, the same man she couldn't wait to see every day at work.

The one she'd hoped for so long would notice her. Now

that he had, she couldn't walk away. No matter what else had happened between them, she considered him a friend.

Letting him brood alone wasn't an option.

After leaving work, Gianna drove the short distance to Shane's condo. She rode the elevator to his floor and stepped out when the doors opened. For so many reasons it was tempting to step right back in. She was more tired than she ever remembered being in her life. It had been a very long day. She could hardly believe that only twenty-four hours ago they'd walked in the snow and he'd kissed her. The battery in her car rolled over, died and Shane drove her home.

Then he'd made love to her—thorough, sweet love.

It had been only this morning they'd had breakfast in her apartment and were intimate, carefree. He'd been relaxed, funny and sweet. Rumpled in the best possible, sexiest way. The thought made her stomach shimmy like it had when the elevator whisked her up to his floor.

The expression on his face when he'd left work a little while ago was so different from this morning. It was a lot like his expression outside the bakery when Allaire commented on his resemblance to Dax and D.J. It was similar, but worse somehow.

And she had to know he was all right.

"Here goes nothing." She squared her shoulders, marched down the hall and rang his bell.

It wasn't answered right away and she was about to push the button again. She was prepared to pitch a tent in the hall if necessary because she had to see him face-to-face. Fortunately he finally opened the door.

"Hi." She lifted her hand in a small wave.

The only way to describe him was ragged. That seemed contradictory since his designer jeans were impeccable so it was more about attitude. His eyes were shadowed and his white cotton shirt untucked. His mouth was tight and the muscle in his jaw jerked. He had a tumbler in his hand with about two fingers of what looked like Scotch in it.

"I'm not very good company, Gianna."

"I'm not here to be entertained."

"Why did you come?"

"You look like a man in desperate need of a hug."

Nothing about him was welcoming, but she stood her ground. For some reason he'd confided things to her. His family might know, too, but they weren't here and she was. Whether he knew it or not, he needed someone and she was it.

"Can I come in?"

He rested his forearm on the doorjamb. "If you were smart, you'd turn around right now. I'm trouble. When it all blows up, you don't want to be close to me."

The devil of it was she *did* want to be close to him. That wasn't something she seemed to be able to change, even though there was every indication this wouldn't end well.

"I'll risk it. Tell me what happened, Shane. Where did you go tonight?"

Blue eyes, dark and assessing, stared into hers for several moments. "You're not going to leave, are you?"

"No."

Reluctantly, he stepped aside to let her in. "Do you want a drink?"

"What are you having?"

"Scotch."

Did she know her liquor or what? Tending bar part-time did that to a girl. "I'll pass."

She followed him into the living room. Unlike the last time here, she wasn't preoccupied with the expensive artwork and spectacular view. Her only concern was Shane.

She watched his shoulders shift restlessly as he stood by the big windows and stared out at the lights on the ski slope.

She moved behind him and put her hand on his arm and felt the muscles tense. "Let's sit."

He nodded and they walked to the couch, then sat side by side, close enough that their thighs brushed. She felt heat and awareness burn through her, but pushed it away. This wasn't about that.

"So, tell me," she said simply.

"I went to see D.J. at the Rib Shack."

"And?"

"We talked."

"Really? You didn't just stare at each other and grunt?" She tried to lighten the mood.

"We joked around." He rested his elbows on his knees, the tumbler of Scotch held loosely in his fingers. "He told me Dax and Allaire used to be married."

"I'd heard that."

"And yet they've managed to work through the past and still be close. Maybe because of the blood connection."

"Possible. Although a lot of siblings don't speak to each other over a lot less than that."

He lifted a shoulder. "Then he told me about what happened a year ago. How Jasper Fowler kidnapped Rose Traub. How everyone thought Swinton was dead."

"Yeah. You can take the girl out of Thunder Canyon, but you can't take Thunder Canyon out of the girl. My mom clued me in. It was pretty sensational."

He met her gaze. "Then he said something that makes me pretty sure his mother is also mine."

Shocked, she stared at him, the misery on his face. "What?"

"Her maiden name was Smith. Grace S. is the name on my birth certificate." His eyes were bleak. "D.J. said there's no way, but I'm almost certain she had an affair with Arthur Swinton and I'm the result."

"Think about this, Shane." She struggled to pull her whirling thoughts together and form a rational statement in order to help him. "Grace Smith is a common name. Is it possible you're jumping to conclusions?"

"Of course. Anything is possible. But the private investigator narrowed down the search criteria and the population of Thunder Canyon isn't that big. It was even smaller all those years ago. When you factor in the strong resemblance between me and the Traubs, that narrows the odds."

Gianna stared at him, trying to make sense of all this. "An affair?"

He nodded. "The whole Traub family believes Arthur Swinton fantasized about their mom, that not having her drove him crazy. To the point where all he could think about was getting even with them."

The implications of that sank in. "If she had his baby, that would challenge every belief they've ever had about their family. And they have the highest possible regard for their mother and her memory."

"I know." His tone was hard, tortured. "It would be so much easier if they were jerks. But I like them, Gianna, all of them. It feels as if we could be good friends, under other circumstances. If I'm right about this, I've got brothers. Another family. You can't have too much, right?" He tried to smile, but it just didn't work.

"Some people would argue that, but I'm not one of them." She blew out a long breath. "What are you going to do about this?"

"There's the question." He dragged his fingers through his hair. "Information like this could tear them apart after they worked hard to be close. I could tell them about my suspicions and they'll hate my guts, destroy any possible connection I might have had with them."

"Or?"

"Keep it to myself."

"And let it tear you apart instead?" Her heart cried out against that. It was an impossible choice.

He looked down, then met her gaze. "How can I trash their mother's memory? Especially at Christmastime?"

"No matter when they hear, news like this will rock their world," she pointed out. "They have a right to know that you might be a brother."

"I don't know if I can do that to them."

"Then you'd have to continue living a lie." Gianna put her hand on his forearm, feeling the warmth of his skin beneath the material of his shirt. It wasn't clear why, but she needed the connection to say what she had to say. "Hiding the truth is just wrong. Take it from me. I lied to you."

There was a spark of heat in his eyes for just a second, then it disappeared. "How big a lie can it be?"

"Not in the same league as keeping information about who you are from Dax and D.J. But I haven't been completely honest, either."

"About what?"

She looked down, not quite able to meet his eyes. "I did have a travel business in New York, but I lost it. Between people booking trips online and the recession costing them jobs and not traveling at all, I couldn't make a go of it. I lost everything."

"I'm sorry, Gianna."

"I'm thirty years old and have to start over, figure out what I want to be when I grow up. Do you have any idea how humiliating it is to have to move home with your parents?"

"You could have told me the truth."

"Saying I was only in town for a short time was just a

way to save face." He hadn't been sure about his long-term plans and it never occurred to her that things between them could get serious. So, here they were. "It was still a lie and I can tell you that I didn't particularly like living with it."

He looked at her for several moments, then his mouth twitched and he started to laugh.

That was unexpected and hit a nerve. "I bared my soul just now. I'm glad you think it's so funny."

"Sweet Gianna." He kissed her softly. Just a brush of his lips that was more promise than passion. "If anyone had told me that I could laugh at anything tonight I'd have said they were crazy."

"Happy to help."

"You have. More than you know." His mouth curved up again. "And you're right. Your lie of omission is nowhere near as bad as my mess." He took her hand in his. "But no one else could have coaxed a smile out of me. I'm glad you're here."

"I hope you still feel that way because I have to say what I think."

"And that is?" His fingers tensed around hers.

"You have to tell Dax and D.J. If you were in their situation, wouldn't you want to know you have a brother?"

"Yes, but—"

"Okay. Whatever their reaction, they have a right to know about this. Otherwise you're forcing them to live a lie, too."

"You have a point." For several moments he looked thoughtful. "Assuming I tell D.J., I wouldn't want to drop that on him until after Presents for Patriots. It's a big event and he's got to be under a lot of stress. That's more important. This secret has waited all these years—it can wait a little longer."

She put her head on his shoulder. "You're a good man, Shane Roarke."

"I'm glad you think so."

She was glad he couldn't see her face, guess how she felt inside. Her stomach was bouncing like a skier who took a tumble down the slope. Just because she believed what she said didn't mean she wasn't scared for him.

This could all go so badly and she would be to blame for convincing him to do it.

Chapter Ten

On Monday night the restaurant was closed so Gianna accepted her mother's invitation to dinner with the whole family. She parked at the curb and saw her sister's minivan already in the driveway.

This was her first holiday at home in a couple of years because she hadn't been able to afford the trip. Her parents knew now about her business failing and money problems, but at the time she'd been too proud to let on. She sat in the car, looking at the Christmas lights lining the roof of the house where she'd grown up. They didn't flash off and on, or do anything high-tech like change color. It was just happy and solid and stable.

Traditional.

The tree stood in the living-room window with white lights and ornaments, some of them made by Gianna and Jackie in school. Lights in the shape of candy canes lined the yard. Santa with sleigh and reindeer stood on the snow in the center.

Tears filled her eyes. She'd missed everyone so much and was looking forward to Christmas with her family. If only Shane was going to be here it would be perfect.

She brushed the moisture from her cheeks, got out of the car, and walked to the front door with the holiday wreath made of ribbons and pine cones.

After knocking, she let herself in. "Hello?"

Her mother walked down the long wooden floor of the entryway and hugged her. "I'm so glad you could make it, sweetheart."

"Me, too, Mom." Breathing in the scent of pine, she looked at the living room on the right and formal dining on the left. The table was covered with a red tablecloth and set for seven and a high chair. There was a poinsettia in the center with Santa Claus candles in brass holders on either side of it. "The house looks great. So festive. And I think I smell a roast?"

"Your nose is right on. Just put your things on the sofa," Susan said, pointing to the hunter-green, floral love seat by the Christmas tree. "Everyone's in the family room. The men are watching Monday Night Football."

"Okay."

Gianna did as directed, then joined the group in the room that always felt like the heart of the home. The kitchen with granite countertops and island opened to the family room with its overstuffed corner group and flat-screen TV.

Ed Garrison was lifting the roast out of the oven. He was tall and trim, with light hair that hid some of the silver streaking it. He had a distinguished look that could have him reading the nightly news on TV if he wasn't the most popular math teacher at Thunder Canyon High. Her mother worked part-time in a gift shop in Old Town and loved it.

The two of them were partners in life and tonight in the kitchen. They were working together to get the roast out of the oven, make mashed potatoes and gravy. She saw her dad's randy touch on her mom's rear. The playful way she pushed his hand away followed by a kiss on his cheek and a look filled with promise for later.

Jackie was following toddler Emily to make sure she only looked and didn't break any of the Christmas decorations. Her husband, Frank, was on the floor with the two boys, wrestling and tickling. The loud and loving scene made Gianna smile.

It also made her ache with missing Shane.

Jackie turned and spotted her in the doorway. "Look who's here."

The children stopped laughing and shrieking to look at her, then they jumped up and started shouting. "Auntie G!"

"Hi, guys." She went down on one knee and braced for impact as the two boys threw themselves into her arms.

Emily followed moments later, doing her best imitation of her older brothers. "Annie G!"

"Hey, baby girl."

She kissed each of them in order of age. Griffin, the dark-haired firstborn. Then Colin, with his lighter hair and sensitive soul. Finally, little Em, her legs and cheeks not as chubby as six months ago when Gianna had come back home.

She met her brother-in-law's gaze over the heads of his children. "Hi, Frank."

"Hey, G." He grinned. "I can't tell you how grateful I am that reinforcements have arrived."

"Are they wearing you out?"

He was a big guy, over six feet, with dark hair and eyes. Hunky and husky. All that firefighter training equipped him for all kinds of emergencies. If anyone could handle this group, it was Frank Blake.

He stood and grinned. "If I could bottle all their energy and sell it, I'd be a billionaire."

"No kidding." She looked at the three still hanging on her. "How are you guys?"

"Hungry," Griff said.

"Me, too," Colin chimed in.

"How's school?" she asked.

"I like recess best."

"Me, too," the little brother added.

The older boy scoffed. "You go to baby school. It's recess all the time."

"Nuh uh." The middle child shot a glare at his older brother. "You're a baby."

Emily held out her arms. "Up."

While their mother tried to referee, Gianna happily obliged her niece and held the little girl close. She breathed in the mingled scents of shampoo and cookies. "I could just eat you up, Em."

Jackie separated her boys. "Go watch the game with your dad."

"But, Mo-om—" Griff stopped when he got the look.

Gianna recognized it and knew her sister had learned from their mother. She wondered whether or not she'd do it, too, if she had kids. Her thoughts went to Shane and her heart ached for him again. So much had happened since he'd cooked for her at his place. He was trying to come to terms with everything he'd learned about himself and the consequences for others if it was revealed.

Now she understood the brooding expression she'd noticed in his eyes, the conflict about family and where he fit in. She'd never experienced that and hoped for the bazillionth time that her advice was sound.

"Dinner's ready," her mother called out.

Those words sent Jackie into field-commander mode. She and Frank rounded up the kids for hand washing then asked Gianna to put Em in the high chair already in the dining room. Like an intricately choreographed ballet, the adults worked together getting children and food to the table at the same time.

Griffin started to take some mashed potatoes and got another look when Jackie said, "Prayer first. Why don't you say it, sweetie?"

He nodded, then bowed his head and linked his fingers. "Thanks, God, for all the food. And for Mommy and Daddy, Grammy and Granddad and Auntie G." He looked at his parents then added reluctantly, "And for Colin and Em. Is that okay?"

"Good job, son."

"That's exactly what I would have said, Griffie." Gianna was surprised the words got past the unexpected logjam of emotion in her throat.

The next few minutes were a flurry of passing dishes, filling plates and making sure everyone had what they needed.

Her mother looked around the table and said, "Okay, everyone, enjoy."

"And if you don't," her father added, "keep it to yourself."

"So, Auntie G.," Jackie took a bite of mashed potatoes and gravy. "I saw Lizzie Traub at the bakery today. She said you and Shane Roarke were in a couple of days ago. Together."

That brought her up short. She'd forgotten how something like that could spread in a small town. Since coming home she hadn't done a thing that was gossip worthy. Until now. "That's right. I wanted to send something to my roommate in New York."

"At lunch you didn't tell us you were seeing him," her sister added.

At lunch Gianna wasn't sure about that herself. She still wasn't sure what they were, but had to tell them something. "I've gotten to know him recently. We're friends."

"Do you like him?" her mother asked.

"Of course. He's great to work for. Funny and charming."

"Mom and I and every female under seventy-five here in Thunder Canyon think he's drop-dead gorgeous," Jackie added. "What's not to like?"

Frank gave her a teasing look, clearly not threatened. "Should I be jealous?"

"If you'd like," his wife said, sass in her voice. "And I'm glad you even thought to be after all these years and three kids."

"Tell me, Gia—" Her father set his fork on his plate as he looked at her. "Do I need to ask him what his intentions are?"

As much as she wanted to know the answer to that question, she shuddered at the thought. "Please, Dad, I'm begging you not to do that."

"There's the reaction I was going for. My work here is done."

"Ed Garrison, you're going straight to hell," her mother scolded.

"Grammy said a bad word." Griffin's expression was angelic and superior because he wasn't the one in trouble.

Gianna was grateful for the diversion, and conversation for the rest of the meal was about other things. She could just listen, laugh, be with loved ones and distracted from worrying about Shane.

Later, after her sister's family had hustled home because of school the next day, Gianna was alone with her mother.

Her father was dozing on the couch in front of the TV. She wanted to hear again about her parents' first meeting.

"Mom? When did you know that Dad was 'the one'?" She was standing by the sink, a dish towel in one hand, wineglass in the other and braced for the personal questions that would follow about Shane. It was worth the risk given how confused she was.

Susan glanced at her husband and smiled lovingly. "I knew almost from the moment we met."

"Really?"

"Yes. There was attraction, of course." Her face went soft and sort of dreamy. "I still remember exactly how it felt. We were in a room full of people at a friend's wedding reception, but he was the only one I saw. And I stopped looking right then."

"It was that way for Jackie and Frank, too? In high school?"

Her mother nodded. "I worried some about them getting married right after graduation because they were so young. But I didn't try to stop her."

"Because of you and Dad?"

"Yes." Concern put creases in her mother's forehead. "Is there something with you and Shane?"

"No. Yes—" The first time she'd met him there'd been a room full of busboys, waitstaff and restaurant employees when Grant Clifton introduced them to the new chef. She'd felt the "wow" thing her mother just described. "Maybe."

Susan took the glass from her and put it in the cupboard. "Sweetheart, I know you've had disappointments. But you'll know when it's right."

"I guess."

Disappointment was a word designed to sugarcoat her catastrophe of a love life. She realized now that time invested didn't make a man less selfish or more right for her. She envied her sister and mother, getting it right the first time.

She wanted a solid relationship like her parents had. She wanted a guy like her brother-in-law. Six months ago she'd met Shane and had a crush on him from afar. Now she knew him, a man who thought of others first. The kind of man who would let the explosive information about who he really was eat him up inside rather than make trouble for the family he believed was his, one that had already been through a lot.

She'd felt that certain something the first time she saw him but…how could she trust her judgment after so much failure?

And more important, could Shane put the missing parts of himself together and find the peace he needed to settle down? That question might be answered after Presents for Patriots tomorrow night. He'd decided to talk to D.J. about his suspicions when the event was over.

Gianna looked around the Rib Shack's main dining room and hardly recognized it. The same historical town mural and sepia-toned pictures were on the walls, but all the tables usually scattered around in the center of the room had been pushed together for work space. People crowded around them and had an assembly line going. At several workstations, volunteers wrapped small electronics and toiletries in red, green, silver and gold Christmas paper, then passed it down for whoever was doing the ribbon.

Piles of presents waited for a volunteer to pick them up for delivery to where brown shipping boxes waited to be filled, addressed and stacked for transport.

Everyone who'd signed up for the event performed a function that utilized their talents as much as possible and her job was to circulate with hors d'oeuvres. She moved back and forth from where the volunteers were working and D.J.'s kitchen, where Shane was deftly balancing an assembly of ingredients, cooking and keeping things warm.

She pushed through the kitchen's double doors where he was working. "How's it going?"

"Good."

Stainless-steel bowls were in front of him, one with a tomato mixture, the other looked like cheese. Trays of sliced, toasted French bread marched up the long counter.

"Are you holding up okay?"

His expression was hooded but tension in his body said he knew she wasn't talking about food preparation, but what was coming after. "I'm made of stern stuff."

"Yes, you are." The only problem was some of that same stuff made up D.J. and Dax Traub. They didn't know yet that their world was going to turn upside down. She hated this and could only imagine how Shane felt. Stiff upper lip. "Everyone is raving about those little pastry things."

One corner of his mouth turned up. "It's a new recipe."

"Talk about a spectacular debut." Chalk up one good thing. "I'll just refill my tray. Hang in there."

She saw him nod and the way the muscle in his cheek moved. He was strung pretty tight and there was nothing to do but wait until this event was over.

After refilling her tray with napkins and food, she moved back out into the big room. The high ceiling held in the hum of voices and laughter. In one corner, the Thunder Canyon radio station was broadcasting Christmas music and live updates from the affair. On the opposite side of the room a TV reporter from a local affiliate was interviewing D. J. Traub, who looked happy, excited and intense. That was probably a family trait because she saw a lot of it in Shane.

She stopped at a table where Angie Anderson and Forrest Traub were working together. Holding out the tray, she said, "Care for a snack?"

"Wow, those look good. What is it?" Angie looked up from the MP3 player and paper she was lining up.

"Crab puffs."

Forrest put a piece of tape on the seam to hold the paper together. He shifted his weight to take the strain off his leg, still healing from the wound he'd sustained in Afghanistan. Better than anyone in the room, this former soldier understood what presents would mean to service personnel stationed in a foreign land at Christmas. He met her gaze and there was a twinkle in his light brown eyes. "You could just leave that whole tray right here if you want."

Angie laughed. "That's the spirit. Pig out for Patriots."

"I have to keep up my strength in order to help out my brothers in arms," he defended.

"Uh-huh. You're a giver, Forrest Traub." Angie put several of the puffs on a napkin. "Thanks, Gianna."

"You're welcome. And, Forrest?" She grinned at the former soldier. "If there are any of these babies left over, they're yours. I'll do my best."

He saluted. "If I wasn't already head over heels in love with Angie…"

"But you are," she reminded him, her voice teasing.

"I definitely am." He met her gaze and there was absolute sincerity in his own.

Gianna sighed as she moved to the next table. Antonia and Clay Traub were doing ribbon duty. She was surprised to see them. "Hey, what are you two doing here?"

Antonia pushed a long, wavy strand of brown hair behind her ear. Green eyes glowed with good humor, but looked a little tired around the edges. "What you really want to know is what have we done with the kids."

"No," Gianna said. "What I really want to know is how

you can possibly look so beautiful and *slim* after giving birth less than two months ago."

Clay gazed at his wife and the love there was clear for everyone to see. A boyishly handsome man with brown eyes, he'd been raising his own six-month-old son when he rented a room at Wright's Way, Antonia's boarding house, when she was in the third trimester of pregnancy. Her plan was to be a single mom, but they fell for each other and got married. Now they were mom *and* dad to two babies.

"She's an amazing mother," Clay said, then kissed his wife's cheek, "and an even more amazing woman."

"And that's my secret," she said, sending the love right back to her husband. "A man who thinks everything I do is perfect."

Gianna held back a sigh. "Okay. Now I want to know what you've done with the kids."

"It's a wonderful invention called grandparents." Clay laughed. "My folks are here from Rust Creek and will stay on through the holidays."

"Ellie and Bob are really good with the babies," Antonia gushed.

"They should be," Clay told her, "after having so many kids of their own."

"Maybe they should hire out," Gianna said, giving them some crab puffs.

If she had babies, her folks would be there for her. They were fantastic grandparents to Jackie's kids but it was looking like that would be it for Susan and Ed Garrison, thanks to the failure of their older daughter to provide any. Envy seemed to be Gianna's new best friend these days. She was jealous of everyone. Everywhere she turned people were deliriously happy and sappy with romance. Was she the only person in the room who had the love carrot dangling in front of her just out of reach?

She moved past more tables where she saw her landlady and husband, Cody Overton. After that came Joss and Jason Traub, who had renovated and updated The Hitching Post. They'd pretended to be a couple and ended up falling in love. Gianna was pretending to be full of holiday spirit but was falling into a funk.

Envy was nothing given the fact that she just wanted to be with Shane. But when she looked at the road ahead for her, all she could see were speed bumps. His biological parents were like a cloud hanging over him and he might not stay in Thunder Canyon.

She had a few hors d'oeuvres left on the tray when she stopped at the place where Dax and D. J. Traub were filling the brown packing boxes with gifts and sealing them with heavy duty tape. Apparently D.J. had finished his interview. Both men straightened and towered over her.

"Hungry?" she asked.

Dax took a napkin and popped one of the seafood-filled pastries into his mouth. "Mmm. What is this?"

"Crab puff," she said without much enthusiasm.

"Good," Dax said after chewing and swallowing. He took another. "Have you been scarfing these down?"

"No. Why?"

"Because you are what you eat and you look crabby."

"He meant thoughtful," D.J. said, glaring at his brother. "Maybe preoccupied. Or pensive."

"No." Dax folded his arms over his chest. "I meant crabby. Where's your Christmas spirit? What's up, G?"

The words yanked Gianna out of her funk with an almost audible snap. She was selfish, shallow and self-centered. These two brothers had no idea that their world was about to tilt. That when the evening ended everything they believed about their mother would be changed forever and not in a good way.

She didn't want to talk about what was bugging her. "Speaking of Christmas, it's only about two weeks away. Will these boxes get to Afghanistan in time?"

"The Air Force National Guard is on Operation Santa Claus," D.J. explained. "They've got transport aircraft standing by to take everything, and staff in place to get it distributed by Christmas."

"Thank goodness," she said.

D.J.'s expression was curious. "Nice try, G. But you didn't answer the question. How come your Christmas spirit is missing in action?"

She forced herself to look them in the eyes. "We're here to do our part to make Christmas merrier for the men and women halfway around the world who are protecting our freedom. Please don't make me feel as shallow as a cookie sheet and admit out loud, here of all places, that I'm feeling sorry for myself."

"Is there a guy involved?" D.J. took the last of the hors d'oeuvres on her tray.

Of course he'd go there. Since she'd been working at the resort restaurant, she'd stopped in the Rib Shack from time to time and D.J. took her under his wing. She'd confessed her pathetic and unfortunate relationship history and his advice was to pick better guys. Talking to him had helped, but now she wished she hadn't. She wasn't sure he wouldn't see through whatever lie she pitched him.

"Oh, you know—"

"The classic non-answer," he said nodding. "That's okay. It's not necessary for me to know details. But you don't have a big brother so I'll do the honors and beat him up for you if necessary."

Oh, God, don't say that, she prayed. She didn't want Shane hit. Not for her and especially not by the man who was his half brother.

"I appreciate the offer, D.J., but I can take care of my-self." At that moment she saw Shane nearby with a tray of bruscetta. Her heart boomeranged in her chest as he took out his reality TV smile and worked everyone over with it. She wasn't immune.

Dax's voice penetrated her haze with a comment that sounded as if he'd just remembered. "You and Shane were out shopping together."

"That's right." D.J. followed her gaze. "You and Shane? What's up, G?"

Good question. One she didn't want to answer. So she asked the first thing that popped into her mind. "What do you think of him?"

The brothers stared at each other for several moments, then Dax said, "His crab puffs are really good."

"Better than the ribs here at the shack?" D.J. challenged.

"Tomato, tomahto." Dax shrugged. "Just saying…"

"Seriously?" Gianna was aware that she was pushing, but this was important. The answer could make a big dif-ference in how they received the news he planned to give them. "You do know I wasn't talking about his cooking skill, right?"

"Well," Dax mused, "he's stepped up every time some-one asked him to pitch in. Thunder Canyon is lucky to have a celebrity who's also not a jerk."

"That's true," she said. "He spent his day off making all the hors d'oeuvres. And tonight The Gallatin Room only took a few reservations from people staying here at the re-sort so that the staff would be free to volunteer for your event. Shane figured most everyone from town would be here and not going out to dinner, anyway."

Dax nodded his approval. "Above and beyond the call of duty."

"I hate to admit my brother is right about anything." D.J.

grinned. "But Shane's willingness to be a part of this town goes a long way toward earning my loyalty. He and I have talked some and he seems like a great guy."

"He is. Really, really is."

Gianna knew her tone was more enthusiastic than necessary when the brothers exchanged a questioning look. This felt a lot like watching an air-disaster movie where she wanted to shout, "Don't get on the plane!"

There was nothing she could do and that was frustrating when she wanted so badly to help everyone involved because she liked, respected and cared about all of them. Shane was going to drop a very big bomb on this family tonight and she didn't want Dax and D. J. Traub to hate him for it.

Chapter Eleven

Gianna had left the Rib Shack a while ago after giving Shane a kiss and hug that went on so long he'd hated to let her go. She'd offered to stay, but this was something he had to do alone. He'd given her the key to his condo when she said sleeping wasn't likely until she knew what happened, and he was grateful to her yet again. If he was being honest, he wasn't sure how he'd have gotten this far without her.

Shane took his place in a line of volunteers who passed the brown cardboard boxes filled with presents into trucks for the next part of the journey to soldiers overseas. After that he pitched in with D.J. and a half dozen other men to move tables and chairs, put the Rib Shack's main dining room back the way it was before being taken over by patriotic holiday elves. At least he was doing something good while killing time waiting to do something not so good.

D.J. inspected the room after he and Shane moved the last table and settled the two chairs on either side. He nodded with satisfaction and announced, "Okay, everyone, I think that does it. Thanks for all your help. I literally could not have done this without you."

Shane watched D.J. shake hands with the men who left through the restaurant doors that led to the public parking lot just outside, which was nearly empty now. He locked up and wearily rubbed the back of his neck.

D.J. turned and seemed to realize he wasn't alone. He looked tired. "Shane— Sorry—I'll unlock the doors if you're going this way."

He was going to hell, but not through those doors. The Rib Shack had a rear entrance just like The Gallatin Room. "No. I'll head out through your kitchen, if that's okay."

"No problem. Would you like a beer? I could sure use one. And a little company would be welcome if you're not too tired."

"I'm used to these hours. Kind of goes with a food-service career," he said. "A beer sounds good."

"Follow me." The other man turned and led the way.

As they walked toward the kitchen, D.J. detoured into the bar and came out with two longnecks. He handed one to Shane, then continued to the back of the restaurant, turning off lights as he went.

He pushed through the double doors and glanced around. Shane knew that look, the one a chef used to make sure there's nothing out of place. To make sure heat sources are shut down, food put away, everything clean. Shane had been the last one in here and followed the other man's gaze.

The long, stainless-steel counter was spotless. Mixing bowls were nested and stacked on shelves. Recently washed pots and pans hung on overhead racks and different size knives back where he'd found them. After doing his volunteer part with the food, Shane had made sure this room was locked down.

"Looks good in here, too. Thanks." D.J. twisted the cap off his beer, then held it out for a toast. "Another successful Presents for Patriots. Here's to pulling it off."

"A job well done, thanks to you." Shane tapped the other man's bottle with his own.

"By the way," D.J. said, "my brother liked the crab puffs."

He's my brother, too, Shane thought. *And so are you.*

He hated this. They were good guys and he was tempted to walk away now, keeping the scandal to himself. But he couldn't fault Gianna's point. If the situation were reversed, he'd want to know. It was the right thing to do.

The timing couldn't be worse, just before Christmas, but there would never be a good time. This wasn't something he wanted overheard and indiscriminately spread around town.

Shane leaned back against the stainless-steel counter and took a long drink of beer. After drawing in a deep breath, he said, "D.J., there's something I need to talk to you about."

"Gianna." The other man nodded knowingly.

"What?"

"I saw the way you two looked at each other tonight."

"Excuse me?"

"My wife is a teacher, as you know. She's educating me in the touchy-feely stuff." He took a drink from his bottle, then leaned back against the cold cook top across from Shane. "Don't tell her I said this, but she's right."

"About?"

"If you watch body language, two people are having a conversation without words. Couple's shorthand, Allaire calls it."

"But Gianna and I aren't a couple."

"That's what all the guys say before they are."

"In my case it's true," Shane protested.

He thought about the sexy redhead constantly and she starred in his dreams. When he wasn't with her, he felt hollow inside and that had never happened to him before. The night he'd spent in her bed was seared in his memory, but he was the son of the town villain. He was pretty sure that was a deal breaker.

D.J. studied him. "Just so you know, I'm Gianna's honorary big brother and I offered to beat you up."

The words were teasing, the sort of banter Shane and his own brother did. Under the circumstances, he hadn't expected to smile, but he did. That only made him angrier about what he had to do.

"Did she take you up on it?" he asked, putting it off just a little longer.

"No. She said she could take care of herself."

"And there's nothing to take care of because we're not a couple."

Since coming to Thunder Canyon, Shane had been careful to not get involved, what with all the baggage he had. Gianna, with her sweetness and light, had made him forget just long enough to slip up. He'd only suggested dinner because it couldn't go anywhere. They were both leaving. But she hadn't been completely honest about going back to New York and he couldn't be sorry. If she'd told him the complete truth, he might have passed up the chance to know her and what a loss that would have been.

"Just don't hurt her," D.J. warned. "I'd really rather not have to hit you."

That was going to change. If only Shane could change who he was. He was doing his level best to keep his feelings in check so he wouldn't have hurting Gianna on his conscience along with deceiving everyone in town who'd welcomed him.

And it was time to quit stalling and say what he had to.

"D.J., there's something I need to tell you—"

The other man's eyes narrowed. "You're looking pretty serious. Did someone die?"

Not yet, but what he was going to say would be the death of something. "I came to Thunder Canyon for a reason—"

"Old news. There was a job opening."

Shane figured the best way to break this was to connect the dots from the beginning. "You said to me last week that Thunder Canyon was lucky to have me, but it's not about luck. I'd been researching this town. When I heard the executive chef position would be available, I contacted Grant Clifton to let him know I was interested. He jumped at the chance after a visit to my Seattle restaurant. Career-wise, coming here wasn't the best move. For me it was about getting answers."

"What are the questions?" D.J. tensed.

"As an infant I was given up for adoption. My adoptive family lives in Los Angeles. Mom and Dad are attorneys. Maggie and Ryan, my sister and brother are also adopted, and also lawyers." He set his half-empty beer bottle on the counter beside him. "I always knew I was loved, but still felt different from them."

"So you're looking for your birth parents." D.J. skipped steps and cut to the chase. "But why Thunder Canyon? This is a small town and pretty far off the beaten path."

"About a year ago my mother gave me all the information she'd received from the social worker at the adoption agency in Montana. I hired a private investigator who narrowed the search parameters to this town."

"Montana is a long way to go for a baby."

"I guess they wanted me to be far removed from the past." Shane shrugged. "My mother loves me enough to let me do what I need to do."

"And you needed to come here."

"I wanted to get some information on my own and the

kind of questions I had wouldn't get answers on a long weekend."

"So you took the job and positioned yourself to gain trust." D.J. finished his beer and still looked anything but relaxed. "Did you find what you were looking for?"

"I know who my father is, but it's not what I was looking for."

"You wouldn't have started this conversation if you didn't want me to know, too."

"I'd rather no one knew but it's not that simple." Shane dragged his fingers through his hair. Again he remembered what Gianna had said. Be a Band-Aid. Do it quick. "The P.I. managed to get a DNA sample and tests were run proving that Arthur Swinton is my biological father."

D.J.'s mouth dropped open, but no words came out. It took several moments for the information to sink in before he finally said, "He's in jail where he belongs."

"I understand why you feel that way." Shane didn't know what else to say except, "I'm sorry for what he did to you."

D.J. shook his head. "Not your apology to make. This is unexpected, I'll admit. But you're not responsible for his actions."

He figured D.J. continued to be in shock. That was the only reason he was still standing there and hadn't abruptly walked out. What Shane had to say next would probably do the trick.

"I found my mother, too. The name on my birth certificate says Grace S. I'm convinced the 'S' is for Smith."

"That's my mother's name, too." D.J.'s dark eyes narrowed angrily. The information sank in too fast for his mind not to have been moving in that direction. "But what you're implying can't be true."

"It is."

"No way. That would mean my mother slept with Arthur

Swinton and that's impossible. She would never have been with a man like that."

"I'm not making this up. Remember what Allaire said about the resemblance between us?"

"It's bull." D.J. slammed his empty beer bottle on the counter and glared. "What's this really about? Money? Is this a shakedown? You want me to pay so you don't spread dirty lies about my mother?"

"I don't need your money." Shane understood the surprise, shock and resulting anger, that his nerves were strung too tight. But he was treading on thin ice, suggesting Shane was like Arthur Swinton. "My family is wealthy and I've made a fortune on my own. That's not what this is about. We're brothers—"

"Get out." D.J. took a step closer. "I don't want to hear another word."

Shane started to argue, wanted to settle this, but he could see by the other man's expression that he'd shut down. He wouldn't listen to reason. Or anything else, for that matter.

"You can throw me out, but it won't change anything." Shane met his gaze, then headed for the back exit.

D.J. followed. "Don't even think about repeating this crap. I won't have my mother's memory and reputation ruined by a pack of lies."

"I don't lie," Shane said quietly. "And if I wanted everyone to know, I would have said something a couple of hours ago in the dining room when the whole town was there."

"I have no idea what sick game you're playing, but I want no part of it." D.J. opened the back door. "Now get out."

Shane nodded and stepped outside. The door shut instantly and he heard the dead bolt slam home. Cold and dark surrounded him.

When this journey of self-discovery started, he'd believed the truth would enlighten him. The real truth was that he'd never felt colder or more in the dark.

As the saying went, one picture was worth a thousand words and the instant Gianna saw Shane's face, she knew that was true. Things with D.J. hadn't gone well.

She'd been pacing in front of the spectacular windows looking out on the ski slope, snow-covered hills and lights but all she could think about was Shane, all alone while doing the hardest thing he'd ever done. As soon as she heard the condo door open, she rushed to meet him in the entryway. He looked tired, defeated. His mouth pulled tight and there was tension in his jaw.

Gianna asked anyway, "How'd it go?"

"Could have been better."

"He didn't take it well."

"How would you interpret getting thrown out of the Rib Shack?"

"Oh, Shane—"

She moved close and put her arms around him. He resisted for half a second, as if he didn't deserve her comfort, then pulled her tighter against him. He buried his face in her neck, breathed in the scent of her hair and held on as if he never wanted to let her go.

"I don't know, Gia—"

He'd never called her that before. He'd always used her full name. Something about the nickname got to her, intimate in a way sharing the pleasure of their bodies hadn't been. Her heart squeezed painfully in a way *it* never had before, and felt as if she'd stepped over the edge into feelings deeper and more profound than she'd ever known.

But she couldn't think about that now. She was simply grateful that he didn't seem angry at her for convincing him to tell D.J. they were half brothers. She hoped that didn't change.

Gianna slipped her arm through his. "Let's go sit in the living room."

He nodded and let her lead him over to the couch. On the coffee table there was a tumbler with two shots of Scotch in it waiting for him.

He kissed her softly and said, "Thank you."

"Anytime." And she sincerely meant that.

With a weary sigh he took the glass and tossed back half the liquor, closing his eyes as it burned all the way to his belly. "I needed that."

Gianna sat on the couch and looked up at him. "What did he say?"

"That it was a lie and I must be trying to shake the family down for money."

She shook her head. "He was just lashing out. This really came out of the blue for him. When it sinks in he'll realize that you don't need the money."

"That's what I told him. More or less." He drank the rest of the Scotch, then sat beside her, close enough that their arms touched and thighs brushed.

"I wouldn't hold it against him, Shane. Anyone would have reacted that way."

"Agreed. That wasn't a surprise. I expected it."

"But you're still upset." It wasn't a question. One look at his face had confirmed his inner turmoil.

"Yeah, I'm upset." He dragged his fingers through his hair. "The thing is... I like him, Gia. And Dax. The whole extended family. We could have been good friends. But now—" The look on his face was tormented. "I have a better chance of opening a restaurant on Mars."

He hadn't expected to be this troubled, she realized. The Traubs hadn't been in his life until a few months ago. But like the town of Thunder Canyon, he'd connected with the family in a way friendship didn't completely explain.

She cared deeply for this man and wished there was a simple, easy way to make his pain disappear. But the only weapon she had was words. Maybe talking it through would help. And she had to know…

"Are you upset with me for pushing you to say something to D.J.?"

"You didn't push me. No one could if I wasn't leaning in that direction in the first place. I'm stubborn that way." He linked his fingers with hers. "And I don't think I could ever be upset with you. I didn't say it before, but I'm glad you're here."

"There's nowhere else I'd be." She leaned her head on his shoulder.

"But," he said, "I can't help thinking that it would be better if I'd just left things alone. Not disturbed the ghosts of the past."

"For what it's worth, I don't think the Traubs are the type to run away from a problem. Seems to me they face things head-on, in a proactive way. Like you did tonight." She looked up at him, the strong profile, determined set of the jaw. "It occurs to me that besides the strong resemblance, that head-on thing is a trait you have in common with them."

"Did you just pay me a compliment?"

"That was my intent, yes." She rubbed her thumb over his. "The point is, and I do have one, regardless of the fallout from all of this, the truth is always best."

"I'm not so sure about that." His voice was soft, sad, with a touch of self-loathing.

She thought carefully about what to say next. "How about looking at this another way."

"I'll take anything I can get."

"Okay, here goes. You already know Arthur is your father."

"Unfortunately, yes."

"This is where I argue that you need an attitude adjustment."

"Oh?"

Gianna knew if she looked at him, one dark eyebrow would be lifted. "Think about it. Whatever combination of DNA made you the way you are is something I'm grateful for. You're a good man. If not, the people of Thunder Canyon would not have embraced you so completely. They're funny that way. And you're awfully pretty to look at."

He laughed, the desired reaction, and hopefully that eased some of his tension. After several moments he sighed. "But the things my father did. He messed with people's lives, stole money. Conspired to commit God knows what kind of felonies."

"All part of the public record. But—" She met his gaze. "You're wondering about bad traits you might have inherited. If you had criminal tendencies, they'd probably have surfaced by now. Have you ever had a run-in with the law?"

"Just a couple of speeding tickets."

"That's so small-time," she scoffed. "And proves my point. The tests confirmed that he's your father. But the evidence is circumstantial that Grace Traub was your mother. Is it possible she's not? That she and Arthur never had a relationship and he is crazy just like everyone thinks?"

"Anything's possible," Shane admitted. "My parents told me everything they know and my mother turned over all the information she has. Grace died years ago. The only way to prove something like that would be a DNA test for Dax, D.J. and me. They'd never agree."

Gianna knew he was right. Grace was gone and couldn't confirm or deny. Dax and D.J.'s father had died, too, so there was no way to even find out if he knew anything. Obviously their children were all in the dark about the past. There must be another way to get the truth besides DNA testing. She just couldn't stand the idea of Shane not being able to know for sure and put this to rest.

If he was the type to let it drop, he never would have undertaken this journey in the first place. If it wasn't so important for him to find the peace to settle down, his mother wouldn't have given him her blessing for the journey that led him to where he was now. Gianna was afraid that not knowing for sure about his biological mother would cost him the piece of himself that he would need to have a life. And that gave her an idea.

"There's someone you haven't talked to yet about this. He might have the answers you're looking for."

Shane's body tensed, the muscle in his arm flexed. "I've talked to everyone I can think of. Who could possibly be left?"

"Your biological father."

"You're joking."

"No. I'm completely serious. Think about it. He's the only key player still alive. The only one who can tell you what really happened."

"But everyone says he's crazy. Delusional. A nut case. And even if he wasn't, there's the whole issue of not being truthful and less than an upstanding citizen."

"He did some bad things," she admitted. "But the Traubs are the most vocal about him being crazy. I think that's about them not wanting to believe their mother could ever have hooked up with a man like Swinton. What if they're wrong? You owe it to yourself to find out the truth."

"Even if I decided to go see him, what makes you think he'd tell me the truth? How could I know for sure whether or not to believe anything that comes out of his mouth?"

"Face-to-face you'd probably get a sense of whether or not he's delusional. The rest…" She shrugged. "I can't see that you've got a choice, Shane. It's the only thing left."

He thought about it for a long time. Finally he looked at her and said, "You're right about me being the type to face problems head-on. Whether or not I find out anything, no one can say I didn't at least try."

Gianna knew he meant himself. He didn't want to look back and hate himself for leaving even one stone unturned.

"I guess we're going to the jail," she said.

He lifted one eyebrow. "What's this 'we' stuff?"

"You don't think I'm letting you go alone, do you?"

There was a fiercely rebellious expression on his face. "This is my problem. More important, I don't want you in a place like that. Yes, I'm going alone."

"Wrong. I'll be there with you."

"I won't allow it," he said.

"At the risk of sounding childish…" She lifted her chin. "You're not the boss of me."

"Actually, I am," he reminded her.

"Only at work. This is different." It was personal.

Her track record proved that when things got personal she was the queen of perseverance.

Chapter Twelve

Shane wasn't sure what he'd expected of the county correctional facility half a day's drive from Thunder Canyon. Even at the holidays, or maybe because it was closing in on Christmas, this place was grim. No decorative lights on the outside. Not a Santa, sleigh, or reindeer in sight. Just a series of buildings enclosed by high concrete walls and law-enforcement personnel dressed in navy pants with contrasting light blue shirts.

With Gianna beside him they walked from the parking lot, then stopped at a guard station to show identification and declare their purpose for being there. Visiting was all Shane said and the guard directed them to the visitor center where they followed signs to a room with scratched tables and battered chairs. There was a surveillance camera mounted on the wall and a big window allowed guards to monitor everything that went on.

A few people were there talking to inmates wearing orange jumpsuits. A sad-looking artificial Christmas tree with a handful of red and green ornaments and tacky gold garland stood in the corner. This was where they'd been instructed to wait while someone went to get Arthur Swinton.

Shane walked to an empty table with three chairs in the farthest corner of the room. Gianna sat beside him and glanced around, blue eyes wide, looking curious and a little apprehensive.

"Scared?" he asked.

"No. You're here."

In spite of this surreal situation, he felt himself smile. "As good as I am with a knife in the kitchen, I'm not sure my skill set would be of much help in a jail riot."

"You've been watching too many prison shows on TV. I don't think this is that kind of place. It's not maximum security." She looked around at the dingy, institutional-green walls. "But we're not in Thunder Canyon anymore."

"I tried to talk you out of this. Are you sorry you came?"

She shook her head and slid her hand into his beneath the table. "Not even a little."

"That makes one of us." He listened to the low murmur of voices and glanced at the two prisoners with multiple tattoos, each talking to a wife or girlfriend. There was a hardness in the eyes, a toughness in the posture and he didn't doubt for a second that either or both could *lead* a prison uprising. These felons were his father's peer group and social contacts.

"I'd rather be anywhere else," he said. "If only I were cooking a five-course meal for a thousand pompous and pretentious food critics who don't know marjoram from parsley. That sounds like a warm and happy good time compared to this."

"Which is why I couldn't let you come here alone."

As much as he'd wanted to protect her from this toxic

environment, Shane was grateful for the stubborn streak that made her dig in and defy him. "Thank you. I appreciate it very much…"

Then the door opened and a uniformed guard walked in with an inmate wearing the same orange jumpsuit that would make it difficult to blend into a nonprison population should Arthur Swinton escape again. Shane's stomach knotted as he studied the prisoner.

His father.

The man was shorter and less significant than he'd expected, slightly built with gray hair. He was probably around sixty, but looked much older.

Since he and Gianna were the only other visitors without an inmate, the man walked over to them and sat down on the other side of the table. His blue eyes were sharp with suspicion.

"Are you Arthur Swinton?" Shane asked.

"Yeah. Do I know you?"

"We've never met. I'm Shane Roarke."

Gianna held out her hand. "Gianna Garrison."

He ignored it. "What do you want?"

"I'm here to ask you some questions."

He sniffed dismissively. "Another reporter. I don't—"

"It's not like that." Shane knew Swinton was referring to the private investigator's cover story when he'd posed as a journalist to get a DNA sample. "Actually I'm a chef in The Gallatin Room at the Thunder Canyon Resort. Gianna is a server there."

He was aware that she hadn't said anything since introducing herself, but knew she was studying both of them, comparing. Searching for a family resemblance. As far as Shane was concerned they looked nothing alike.

"What do you want?" Swinton asked again. The introductions hadn't done anything but deepen his distrust.

"I'd like to know about you and Grace Smith—you might know her as Grace Traub."

"She'll always be Grace Smith to me." Something that sounded a lot like sorrow took the sharp edge out of his voice. "What about her?"

"Obviously you knew her?"

"Yeah."

"Did you date her?"

"Yeah."

This was like pulling teeth, Shane thought, feeling frustration expand in his gut. Just then Gianna squeezed his hand, as if she knew what was going on inside him. It kept him focused. Allowed him to see that self-preservation was instinctive in a place like this. In navigating the criminal-justice system, offenders learned not to trust or give up anything that might incriminate them.

"There's no reason you should believe me," Shane assured him, "but I'm not here to do you any harm. I just want information about the past."

"Me and Grace."

"That's right." He stared hard into blue eyes that seemed familiar. "Were the two of you close?"

"You're asking if I slept with her. Not that it's any of your business or anyone else's. No one believed it then, why should you now?" The man was nothing if not direct. There was a vacant look on his face, as if he were remembering something from a long time ago. And apparently he wanted to tell his story because he added, "I slept with her, but it wasn't just sex. Grace is the only woman I've ever loved."

The guy had no idea who he was. As far as Shane could see, he had no reason to lie about that, but the admission profoundly shocked him. Probably because every time Swinton's name came up in Thunder Canyon it was in a negative context painting him as a heartless, unprincipled nut case who was incapable of deep feeling.

"Why did you break if off?" Shane asked.

"Of course I'm the bad guy." That was an ironic comment since he was the one in prison, but Swinton's gray eyebrows pulled together. "Who told you I did?"

"No one. I just—" Shane figured he was a heartless nut job.

"Gracie broke up with me. I tried to get her to reconsider, but she swore it was over." He took a deep, shuddering breath. "Her folks didn't like me much and Doug Traub was interested in her. They thought he walked on water."

So far the man hadn't said anything that convinced him Grace was his mother.

"She started going out with Doug?" Shane prodded.

"Not right away. At least not that I knew. I tried to see her, but her folks wouldn't tell me where she was."

When Gianna's hand tightened on his, Shane looked at her and knew they were thinking the same thing. Had she been sent away to hide a pregnancy? "She left town?"

"Yeah."

"But she came back."

"About six months later," he confirmed.

"Did she tell you why she went away?" His heart was pounding.

"Hell, no. She wouldn't even look at me, let alone be caught in a conversation."

Out of guilt? Shane wondered. Did her parents pressure her to keep quiet? Because it was sure looking like she was pregnant with Swinton's baby and didn't tell him.

"What did you do?"

"I kept trying to call her, see her, tell her I loved her. Then it was all over Thunder Canyon that she was dating Doug Traub. Next thing I knew she was engaged to him."

His hands clenched into fists on the table, right beside the word "hell" carved on the top. "She was making a mistake and I couldn't get past her father or Traub to make her see what she was doing."

Shane could feel the man's pain and didn't know what to say. This part of the story was history. "She married him."

"Yes." Swinton snapped out the single word. It was rife with bitterness, and sadness etched lines in his craggy face. "Then she died. So damn young. I hated that I didn't get time with her. The Traubs had her all to themselves. I never got to tell her I'll always love her. Never got to say goodbye."

"Mr. Swinton—" When Gianna finally spoke up, her voice was gentle. "Is that why you were trying to ruin the Traubs? To get even because you were shut out?"

"They had everything. I had nothing. It kept eating at me."

"But they're Grace's children."

He looked down, miserable and unhappy. "She'd hate me for it and I'm sorry for that." He looked sorry. "Grief does crazy things to a man. I was desperate for a way to get out from under it."

Shane studied the man. He looked alternately sad, angry and lonely, but not crazy. Loving a woman who didn't return his feelings had started him down a path of bitterness that led to a series of crimes that were all about revenge against the family he blamed for a lifetime of unhappiness. But he wasn't the only one with a black mark.

Grace Smith never told this man that she was pregnant with his child. Shane couldn't help wondering if knowing would have made a difference.

Swinton shook his head sadly. "I thought being left out in the cold was bad, but it's nothing compared to not having Gracie on this earth at all. Now I've got no one."

When Gianna squeezed his hand, Shane looked at her

and saw a slight nod. He knew what she was saying and agreed. "It's not entirely true that you have no family."

The suspicion ever present in the man's expression now turned to bitterness. "What are you talking about?"

"I'm your son. Yours and Grace's."

Blue eyes narrowed and turned angry. "If this is some scheme to get money out of me, you can just shove it—"

"No." Shane held up his hands in a take-it-down-a-notch gesture. Why was it that everyone accused him of a scam when his only goal was to get at the truth? "I had a DNA test."

"You didn't get a sample from me."

"Yeah, I did. Remember that reporter who came to see you?" There was a slight nod along with an expression that said he was wondering how Shane could know that. "He's a private investigator. I hired him to get a sample from you. The test results show to a ninety-nine percent certainty that you're my biological father."

"Is this some kind of sick joke, because I don't think it's funny."

"Tell me about it. You're in jail. I have restaurants in big cities across the country. This is not the kind of thing that would help my business. What possible good would making up this connection do me? My reputation could be ruined. The fact is that you *are* my father."

After several moments the old man's expression softened as the truth of the words sank in. "You're my son? Mine and Gracie's?"

"That's what I believe, yes."

"I have a son?" He stared across the table and didn't look quite so old and broken. "I can't believe it. I have a son."

Gianna looked at Shane, then his father. "You're not physically alike, but the eyes are the same, in shape, color and intensity."

"I didn't know she was pregnant. So that's why she went away. This is amazing. I don't know what to say. You're a part of me and Grace." He started to reach for Shane's hand, then stopped. "I don't know what to do. What's right. Sorry. I can hardly wrap my head around all of this."

Shane understood exactly what he was saying because he'd just confirmed the worst. He was the son of the man who was serving time in jail for crimes against Thunder Canyon and the Traub family.

His family, although they would reject that.

What the hell was he going to do?

"Shane, say *something*. You're starting to scare me."

Truthfully, the dark expression on his face had scared Gianna twenty miles ago, when they'd driven away from the jail. Now his chronic silence had her approaching frantic. She glanced at him, then turned the radio volume down.

He kept his eyes on the long, straight road. Most of the snow had melted, but there were still pockets of white where tree trunks and bushes shaded and protected it from direct sunlight. His hands gripped the wheel so tightly, she expected it to snap any second.

"I don't have anything to say."

"That's impossible. You just met your birth father for the first time." She didn't add that it was in jail, but knew he was thinking it, too. "I'm not buying the fact that you've got nothing."

"What do you want to hear?"

Stubborn, exasperating man. If she were bigger and he wasn't so tall, broad and muscular, she'd shake him.

"I don't have a script for you." She studied his profile, the lean cheek and stubborn jaw. There must be feelings, impressions—*something*—rolling around in his head. From the look of his expression, the thoughts were pretty dark. "Tell me what you're thinking."

"It's a nice day for a drive."

She sighed and shook her head. "Don't make me hurt you."

"So, you do have a script. Or a list of acceptable subjects."

"Not so much that as a specific topic," she said. Maybe questions would draw him out. "What did you think of him?"

"Arthur?"

Okay. He wasn't going to call the man dad. "Yes. Arthur."

"He's pretty intense."

So are you, she wanted to say, but decided he wasn't in the mood for a DNA characteristics comparison spreadsheet. It might get him to open up if she shared her impressions.

"I sort of expected him to look, I don't know, edgier somehow. More convict tough. Kind of like a hardened criminal."

"He's an old man." That sounded like he agreed with her and there was the tiniest bit of pity in his tone.

"Did it seem to you like he was telling the truth?"

"You mean do I think he's crazy?" Shane glanced at her. "No. He's a lot of things, but crazy isn't one of them."

"So you believe he and Grace were involved? That she left Thunder Canyon to give birth?"

He nodded without meeting her gaze. "Yeah, I do. I'm all but certain that Grace Smith Traub was my mother."

She was glad he knew the truth, but it also made her sad. After all his efforts to find his birth parents now he'd discovered his father in jail and his mother had died. It all seemed like a cruel twist of fate.

"So you'll never have a chance to know her."

"Not face-to-face."

She knew what he was saying. Grace had died when they were pretty young, but her sons, his half brothers, could share memories of their mother. "You could talk to Dax and D.J. about her."

"Not likely." He pulled off the road when a service station, convenience store and diner came into view. "I'm going to get gas. Are you hungry?"

Not really, but it was way past lunch and both of them needed food. "I could eat."

He nodded and parked by one of the pumps, then fueled up. Gianna watched his face as he worked and knew by the shadows swirling in his eyes that the surface of his feelings hadn't even been scratched yet. When he opened the driver's-side door and got in, cold air came with him and she shivered, but that was more about the emotional morning than winter in Montana.

He started the car and drove around the building and parked in front of the Pit Stop Diner. The windows were painted with snowflakes, a Christmas tree and other traditional signs of the season, with a big "Happy Holidays" in the middle. There weren't any cars in the parking lot, so it was no surprise when they walked in to find the place empty.

A thirtyish waitress wearing jeans, a Santa Claus sweatshirt and jingle bell earrings greeted them. Her name tag read Jamee. "Merry Christmas, folks. Sit anywhere."

"Thanks." Gianna picked a booth by the window and sat on the red plastic bench seat. The menus were tucked behind the salt and pepper shakers and the napkin holder. "May I have a cup of tea, please?"

"Sure thing." Jamee stared at Shane as if she were trying to place him, then there was a glimmer of recognition. "Wow. You're Shane Roarke."

"Guilty as charged."

"Wait till I tell Carl." She cocked a thumb toward the counter with swivel stools and the kitchen beyond. "He's the cook here. No pressure, huh?"

Shane smiled and only someone who knew him could tell his effortless charm was missing in action and his heart wasn't in it. "I'm sure the food is great."

She took a pencil from behind her ear and held a pad. "What are you doing all the way out here in the middle of nowhere?"

There wasn't much around except the jail compound they'd been to and Gianna was pretty sure he wouldn't want to share that he'd just visited his father there. She was at a loss with an answer, but Shane handled it with ease.

"I'm working at Thunder Canyon Resort, The Gallatin Room. I wanted to take a drive, clear my head." He looked across the table. "Gianna works with me and kept me company for some sightseeing."

"Not a lot to look at, but I'm glad you stopped in. I'm a big fan. Never missed an episode of *If You Can't Stand the Heat*." Jamee was gushing now and who could blame her? Of all the diners in all the world, a celebrity had just walked into hers. "I voted for you every week."

"I appreciate that."

"You're a lot better looking in person."

"Thanks." The brooding expression was back and pretty easy to read. He was thinking that probably his looks came from his mother because of the strong resemblance to Dax and D. J. Traub. "I think I'll just have a burger. Medium."

"That comes with fries."

"Fine," he said.

"Me, too, and a cup of tea." Gianna grabbed a couple of napkins from the container and put one in her lap.

"Coming right up."

She watched the waitress disappear through a swinging door, then met Shane's gaze. There was doubt, questions and confusion in his eyes and her heart ached for him. She wished she could wave a magic wand and take it all away.

"What are you thinking?" she asked.

His mouth tightened and anger took over his features. "How could she not tell him she was pregnant with his child?"

"I don't know." Gianna knew the "she" in question was Grace. "She was probably scared. It sounds like her parents were strict and controlling."

"It was wrong."

"I can't argue with you there. Arthur had a right to know. Just like Dax and D.J. have a right to know they have a half brother."

"To share memories of their mother with?" His tone was mocking. "That's not going to happen. D.J. made himself pretty clear. They don't want anything to do with me. My very existence puts a big bad ding in her perfect reputation and their memories."

She wasn't so sure he was wrong about that. "Who knew Arthur Swinton would turn out to be the injured party in all this?"

"Injured?" The single word was spoken in a soft, scornful voice. "That implies something he could recuperate from. She ripped his heart out and he never recovered. He fell in love and it ruined his life."

Just then the waitress brought their burgers and fries and set the plates down. "I'll get your hot tea right out. Anything to drink for you?" she asked Shane.

"Not unless you've got something stronger than coffee."

"Sorry." Jamee looked it. "Anything else?"

A miracle, Gianna thought. All she said was, "This is fine."

Her stomach was in knots and there was no way she'd get this or anything else down. Shane was slipping away. She could feel it and there was nothing she could do to stop it.

Leaving her food untouched, she stared across the table. "Shane, look at it from Dax and D.J.'s point of view. This has rocked your world and you always knew you were adopted. The Traubs are just finding out their mother had secrets. Give them time to process what's going on. You, too. Now you know what happened. You'll come to terms with the past."

"There's nothing to come to terms with." He shrugged. "I found out what I wanted to know. It's over."

That sounded so final. As if he was finished with a part of his life, the part that included her.

"What are you going to do?" she asked.

"It's the holidays. I need to see my family. The one that actually *does* want me around," he clarified. "I'm going to Los Angeles."

She had a bad feeling about this. Just the way he said it made her want to put a finer point on his plans. December 25th was a little over a week away and he was making a trip sound imminent. "For Christmas?"

He shook his head. "As soon as I can get a flight out."

"But that's earlier than you planned." Duh, stating the obvious.

He shook his head. "I never should have started any of this in the first place. If I just go away quietly, the Traubs can get on with their lives and Grace's memory will be preserved."

"But it's not the truth. She was human. She had flaws and made mistakes. That doesn't mean she was a bad person and they shouldn't love her. Or you."

He went on as if he hadn't heard her. "D.J. is the only one who knows. He probably didn't say anything to the rest of them because he didn't believe me, anyway. It's time for me to move on. Like you said, I found out what I came here for."

But was that all he'd found? What about her? What about the two of them? Neither of those were questions she could ask. Instead she said, "What about the restaurant?"

"The sous-chef can take over for me. I've trained her. No one is irreplaceable."

He was wrong about that. He couldn't be replaced in her heart. And that's when she knew she'd fallen in love with him. It was implied when she'd told him there was nowhere else she'd rather be than with him, even meeting his father for the first time in jail. And no matter that he denied it, she was pretty sure he blamed her for convincing him to tell D.J. the truth. The look on his face said he wouldn't forgive her, either.

She'd wasted years on relationships that were wrong and not long at all on one that she'd thought was right, only to find out it was one-sided. He'd connected the dots of who he was and his contract at The Gallatin Room was almost up. So, he had no reason to stay and every reason to go back to Los Angeles.

Somehow it was no comfort that she hadn't put in a lot of time falling for him. Fate had a way of evening the score and she was going to spend the rest of her life missing him.

Chapter Thirteen

In her apartment after work, Gianna took her cup of tea and walked over to the tiny Christmas tree on a table in front of her window. She'd changed out of her work clothes and put on fleece pajama bottoms and a red Henley top for warmth. It was a schleppy outfit, but what did it matter? No one was coming, and by no one she meant Shane. He was either in Los Angeles or on his way.

Between her regular time off and The Gallatin Room's Monday closure she hadn't seen him for a couple of days. Tonight when she'd gone to work Bonnie had broken the news that Shane told the staff he was leaving for the holidays. It felt as if he'd whipped her heart with a wire whisk. The rest of the staff thought he'd be back to work after New Year's, but Gianna knew better.

He was gone for good.

The last couple of days had given her a sad and painful preview of how life without Shane would feel. It was as if someone turned off a light inside her and not even holiday decorations could power it back up.

"The most wonderful time of the year, my backside," she mumbled to herself.

She set her steaming mug on the table where the tree stood and looked at the assembled presents. The packages for her family were arranged on the floor, too big to fit underneath in the traditional spot. Only one was small enough and the tag had Shane's name on it.

She picked up the square box wrapped in gold foil paper with red holly berries. She'd spent a long time getting the three-dimensional red bow just right. That investment of energy was nothing compared to how she'd agonized over what to buy for the man who had everything. Aftershave was a cliché. He didn't wear neckties—also a cliché. Nothing too personal—even though they'd made love and things didn't get much more personal than that. Her body ached with the memories of that magic night, doomed to be a single, life-changing event.

Of course she hadn't known that when picking out his present. It couldn't be too expensive, mostly because her budget would only stretch so far. But still the gift had to mean something.

She looked at the box holding the blue wool neck scarf that matched his eyes. "It means I'm an idiot."

He was gone and she should give this to charity so someone could use it.

Then she realized she *was* the charity case who could use it. "For a horrible warning to never fall in love again."

A knock on the door startled her because it was late and she wasn't expecting anyone. Her family would have called. No one would just drop in unless it was someone who knew her schedule. Someone like Shane.

Her heart started to pound and she walked to the door,

then peeked out the window beside it. He was there on the landing and the light that had gone dark inside her blazed brightly again. He was here; he hadn't left town. He was...

What? Her hands shook as she looked at the box she was still holding. How quickly the horrible warning was forgotten. But, she realized, the warning was too late, anyway, since she was already in love with him.

She opened the door and the outside cold made her shiver. His coat was open and his hands were in the pockets. He could really use a scarf to keep him warm.

"Shane. What are you doing here?"

His gaze dropped to her fleece pants and long-sleeved shirt. Maybe it was wishful thinking, but his eyes seemed to go intense for just a moment while lingering on her chest. "I saw your light was still on."

"I thought you'd left town. That's what they told me at the restaurant." Could he tell how hurt she was?

"I had a flight out tonight," he admitted. "I actually made it all the way to the airport, but it felt wrong."

"Define 'it.'"

"Can I come in? Would that be all right?"

No, it wasn't all right. This was like grinding his heel into her already broken heart, but closing the door in his face wasn't an option. And it was too cold to stand here.

She pulled the door wide. "Come in."

"Thanks. I won't stay long."

As he moved past her the air stirred with the spicy masculine scent of his skin and she knew forever wouldn't be long enough for him to stay. But she had no illusions about that wish coming true.

She closed the door and said, "I'm just having some tea. Would you like a cup?"

"No."

She picked up her mug and sat on the sofa, leaving room for him beside her. "So, why are you here?"

"I just wanted to talk to—" He stopped, then slid into the space next to her without taking off his coat. "We're friends, Gianna."

"I thought so." Even she could hear the hurt in her voice.

"I've been an ass and having a lot on my mind is no excuse. I thought going to L.A. would help me sort things out. Then I got to the airport and couldn't go. I've sort of gotten used to talking to you and it was unprofessional to leave the restaurant on short notice."

"What about D.J.?"

"So far I haven't heard anything from him. If there's any fallout from what I said, I'll be here to face it. I'm not hiding."

She nodded approval. "There are no more secrets and that's the way it should be. It's a good plan, Shane."

"It feels good." He met her gaze. "And I don't think I ever told you just how much I appreciate your support through everything. You didn't just listen. You were there for me."

She saw the light dim in his eyes and knew he was talking about that day at the jail. The day his father found out he had a son and the woman he'd loved all his life had kept that from him.

Friendship wasn't nearly enough for her, she thought, but it looked like that was all he was offering and she'd take what she could get. She stared at him to memorize the shape of his nose, the stubborn line of his jaw, the exact shade of blue in his eyes.

"I couldn't let you go to the jail alone," she said. "It's not what friends do."

He looked like he wanted to say something to that, but shook his head and let it go. "Anyway, I had another reason for stopping by."

She felt something quiver inside her and knew it was hope stirring. If she could slap it around and discourage the emotion she would, but that was hard when hope had a life of its own.

"Oh?"

"Yeah. I know you want to travel."

"It was a dream." She was surprised he remembered. "I was always told to study what you love in school. Do what you love in your job. I was good at business and marketing and wanted to see the world. A travel agency seemed like a perfect fit." She shrugged. "It was just a cruel twist of fate that I never got to go anywhere."

"Well, it's not the world, but I'd like to take you to L.A. for Christmas. You've been supportive of me through this weird, crazy, biological-parent journey and I'd very much like you to meet my real family."

"I'm sure they're wonderful people. How could they not be? They raised you and you're a very good man. I wish I could…"

He frowned. "I hear a but."

She squeezed the mug in her hands tightly. "This is my first Christmas with my family in a couple of years. I couldn't afford the trip from New York. I was trying to keep my business afloat and after I lost it, jobs were hard to find. Keeping a roof over my head was important and the city is a pricey place to live. I didn't have the money."

"You couldn't foresee what a toll the recession would take. A lot of businesses didn't make it. Not your fault."

She met his gaze and realized talking to him about her career disaster didn't embarrass her. Even though he was so phenomenally successful, he'd never made her feel less because she didn't hit it big. She appreciated that. "Anyway, this Christmas is all about reconnecting with my folks, my sister, my nephews and niece."

"I understand the importance of family in a very profound way." He was quiet for several moments, thinking. "I'm also not a man who gracefully takes no for an answer."

"Oh?"

"If so, I wouldn't have annihilated my reality show cooking competition by making an edible dish out of beef jerky, kidney beans and wine."

"Eww." She stared at him. "You're joking."

"Only about the jerky." He grinned. "Not about giving up easily. How about a compromise? You have Christmas Eve with your family. I'll take you to L.A. on Christmas day to meet mine."

She didn't like the idea of him being alone for any part of the holiday. "Do you have anywhere to go on the 24th?"

"No, but that's okay." He shrugged. "I'll manage."

"That's just wrong." She couldn't hold back the words. "I'm sure there's room for one more at the Garrisons."

"I wouldn't want to impose," he said.

"My family would love to meet you."

"I'd like to meet them. On one condition," he said. "Come with me to the west coast on Christmas. You've been an incredible friend, more than I deserve. Let me thank you for all you've done. I only want to hear a yes."

And she wanted to hear him say he loved her, but that wasn't going to happen. He was only interested in friendship and she understood why, because she'd been there when he met Arthur Swinton. Love ruined the man's life and Shane wasn't going to let that happen to him.

Where was a horrible warning when you really needed it? If she was smart, she'd tell him no. But she wasn't smart because she couldn't say it. She didn't want the light inside to go out sooner than necessary. Whatever time she had with him she would take, if only to store up memories for when she was alone.

"You win, but then you always do. I'd love to go to Los Angeles with you."

After following Gianna's directions, Shane pulled the car to a stop at the curb in front of her parents' house at the appointed time on Christmas Eve. Her gifts were in the backseat next to a pile that he'd brought. He'd quizzed her about the kids' ages, likes and dislikes, then shopped so he didn't come empty-handed.

He was in a great mood. To her knowledge, in the days since he'd postponed his trip to Los Angeles, he hadn't heard anything from D. J. Traub. Shane hadn't told her how he felt about it and she wasn't going to ask tonight. He wasn't brooding anymore and that was good enough for her.

Gianna removed her seat belt. "Do your brother or sister have any kids?"

"No."

"Can I assume that your career hasn't afforded you the opportunity to spend time with children?"

"That's an accurate assumption." There was a big dose of amusement in his tone.

"Then I have to ask, are you sure you really want to go in there? I love them with every fiber of my being, but they're loud. Probably sugar and any number of chemical food dyes have amped up their normally high energy level. The night before Santa Claus comes there's only peace on earth when they fall into an involuntary, exhausted sleep."

"Are you trying to scare me?" He opened his car door, and the overhead light illuminated his wry expression.

"Just keeping it real in case you want to beat a hasty retreat." She pointed to the driveway. "See that minivan? It means they're already here and waiting to pounce."

"Then let's go join the party."

"Don't say I didn't warn you." She got out of the car then retrieved her presents from the back.

Arms loaded with gifts, they walked to the front door and Shane managed to ring the bell with his elbow. Moments later it was opened and Griffin stood there.

"Auntie G is here," he announced in an exceptionally loud voice.

"Hi, Griff. You know," she teased, "I think there are some people a few streets over who didn't hear you."

"You're funny." He gave Shane a long, assessing look. "Is he your friend?"

She winced at the word, but probably her mother had told him that. "Yes. This is Shane Roarke. My boss. Shane, this is Griffin, my nephew."

"Nice to meet you, Griffin."

"You're the cook?"

"Chef," she corrected.

"What's the difference? Does he cook food?"

"Yes," Shane answered.

"My dad is a good cook. So is Grammy."

"We're coming in now, Griffie." She kissed the top of his head on the way to pile gifts under the living-room tree. "It smells good in here. Turkey, yum."

Griffin stared at the exquisitely wrapped boxes Shane put beside hers. "Did you bring me something?"

"Griffin, it's rude to ask that," she scolded.

"But I wanna know. How am I gonna know if I don't ask? Mommy says it's good to ask questions."

"Your mom is right," Shane said. "And the answer is yes, I did bring you something."

The boy grinned. "Can I open it now?"

"Let's go talk to Grammy and find out what the plan is."

"Okay." He grabbed Shane's hand. "I'll show you where she is."

"Lead the way." Shane whispered in her ear. "Retail bribery works every time."

When they walked into the combination kitchen/family room, the boy stopped. "Auntie G is here and Shane brought us presents. Can we open 'em, Grammy?"

Colin left his fire truck and toy firefighter figures on the rug in front of the TV and ran over to give her a hug. "Hi, Auntie G."

Right behind him was Emily, trying to keep up on her short, pudgy legs, saying, "Annie G!"

Gianna grabbed her up and spread kisses over her cheek until the little girl giggled. "Hey, baby girl. You smell like sugar cookies."

"Cookie." She held up her sticky, crumb-covered hands for inspection. Then she spotted Shane, who grinned at her. Apparently his charm translated to women of all ages because the normally shy-of-strangers child held out her arms to him. "Pick me up."

Jackie rushed over. "You don't have to take her. With those dirty hands she'll ruin your sweater."

It looked like cashmere, a cream color that wouldn't hold up well to grubby hands, Gianna thought. "This is my sister and her husband, Frank."

The two men shook hands, then she introduced her parents. "Shane Roarke, Susan and Ed Garrison."

Her father shook his hand and her mother smiled. "We're so glad you could join us for dinner, Shane."

"Thank you for including me."

"Any friend of my daughter's…" Her father had no idea how that touched a nerve.

Gianna decided for tonight she was not going to let that word get to her. "I smell mulled wine."

"On the stove." Her dad raised his voice to be heard over Emily's wailing.

"Pick me up!" Apparently oblivious to the fact that she was up, the little girl kept holding her arms out to Shane.

"Dirty hands don't scare me. Obviously it's early child-hood training for a career in the food-service industry." He took the child who pointed into the family room. "I guess we're going that way."

While Em chattered to him in a language only a two-year-old could understand, he carried her to the pile of toys on the family-room floor. When he set her down, she grabbed a ragged plastic doll with all the clothes removed and pointed to the face.

"Eye," he said.

"Eye," Em repeated.

Gianna watched as he patiently played the naming-the-limbs game until the boys moved in to get his attention. Frank tried to run interference, but apparently two grown men were no match for three small children. The toys were forgotten in favor of wrestling, tickling and roughhousing. Shane easily went from instigator to casualty, alternately taking one of the boys on his back to letting them tackle him. Jackie and her dad tried to play referee, but no one was listening to them.

Her mother handed Gianna a glass of wine. "He's even better-looking than on TV."

"Am I the only one on the planet who never saw that show?" She was remembering the woman in the middle-of-nowhere diner who'd recognized him. The man playing with her nephews and niece was much different from the shell-shocked one who had just found his birth father.

"Apparently you are," Susan said. "He's a wizard with food and if I weren't so secure in my cooking skills, having a world-famous chef to dinner could be just a little bit intimidating."

"Your turkey is the best, Mom."

"You have to say that, sweetheart, but I appreciate the sentiment."

"It's the absolute truth."

"You were looking pensive just now." Her mother studied her face. "What are you thinking?"

"Just that Shane looks really happy and relaxed."

Susan glanced at the rowdy group with Shane in the center of it. "If that's noteworthy, it would seem he's lately been just the opposite."

This wasn't her story to tell so Gianna gave the heavily edited version. "He's had a lot on his mind lately, but I think the weight has finally lifted from his shoulders." When one of the boys climbed on his back, she laughed. "He's got Colin there now."

"Yes, he does. Also noteworthy is that the kids took to him right away." Susan was using her mother's-seal-of-approval voice. "They have a finely tuned BS—bad stuff—meter and can see through phoniness instantly."

Gianna could read through the lines and the same thought had already crossed her mind. He would make a wonderful father. Tears burned her eyes because no matter how determined she was to put the "friend thing" out of her mind, it would take a Christmas miracle to pull that off.

She ached to be more than that because he was everything she'd ever wanted.

"I like your family." Shane braked at a stoplight a few minutes after leaving the crazy, wonderful Christmas chaos at the Garrison house.

"I do, too," she said. "My mother thinks you're better-looking in person than on TV."

"Good to know." He was feeling a little reflective. "They make me miss my family."

"You'll be seeing them tomorrow."

"As will you."

He glanced at her in the passenger seat, streetlights making her red hair glow. God, he wanted her. In every way. How could he ever have considered leaving her at Christmas?

"Speaking of that," she said, "what time are you picking me up to go to the airport tomorrow?"

"Are you packed?"

"Are you kidding? This is me. I've been packed for a couple days. All ready except for the last-minute things."

That's all he needed to hear. "Then I'm not picking you up."

"Okay." She slid a puzzled glance across the leather console between them. "Do you want me to come by your place?"

"That won't be necessary."

She frowned. "If you changed your mind about me going with you—"

"Just the opposite." He accelerated when the light turned green and passed the street for her place. "Technically I won't need to pick you up because I'm taking you home with me tonight. We can get your things tomorrow on the way to the airport."

It was quiet on the passenger side for so long that he looked over. Gianna was staring at him.

Maybe he'd blown his chance with her after all, but every part of him fought against that. It couldn't be too late. "Do you want me to take you home now?"

"No," she said emphatically. "It's just that I'm confused. You pulled back— I thought— You said we're friends."

"About that—" It felt like he'd been in a fog for months,

a haze that just now cleared. "After seeing Arthur, I guess I went a little crazy. Like father, like son."

"It's called processing the information," she defended.

Loyalty and support were two of his favorite things about her. "In my case it was more about going to the bad place and moving in for a while." He looked over and saw her watching him intently. "I started ticking off the things about me that are like him, none of them good."

"Shane, he has positive qualities. And you didn't get all your DNA from him. You didn't know Grace, but look at her children. They're all good men. Salt of the earth."

"I know. I've thought a lot about everything and had to work it through. Just because he buckled under the weight of disappointment doesn't mean I will."

"That's right," she agreed. "He's not a bad man, I don't think. Just one who lost his way."

"So did I. For a while." Almost to his place, he took her hand while keeping his other on the steering wheel. "Now I've got my head on straight."

She squeezed his fingers. "I'm glad."

He pulled the car into the parking garage and guided it into his space. After getting out, he went to the passenger side and opened Gianna's door, then held out his hand. "Do you mind if we unload the gifts in the morning?"

He'd missed her more than he thought possible and was in kind of a hurry to get her inside. Besides, he had a lot to make up for.

"I don't mind at all." Her expressive eyes hid nothing and promised everything.

She took his breath away.

They went into the elevator and pushed the button for his floor, then walked down the hall to his place where he unlocked the door and led her inside.

"Alone at last," he said, taking her face in his hands. "You're cold."

"Not for long. And my mom gave me something." She reached into her pocket and pulled out a red-ribbon-trimmed sprig. "Mistletoe. Sometimes a girl has to take matters into her own hands."

She held it up as high as she could to get it over their heads. He took it from her and did the job as she slid her arms around his neck.

Need exploded through him as she touched her mouth to his, then pushed at his jacket, trying to get it off. In a frenzy of kissing and wanting he dropped the mistletoe because he needed both hands. They tugged at buttons and closures until coats and keys were on the floor and the raspy sound of their breathing filled the entryway. He could hardly wait to have her, but not here, not up against the wall.

Shane swept her into his arms and laughed at her shriek of surprise. "You know it's Christmas Eve and Santa won't bring presents until you're in bed."

She grinned. "Then what are you waiting for?"

"Not a damn thing."

He carried her to his room where they undressed each other then fell on the mattress in a tangle of arms, legs and laughter. He hadn't realized how lonely the past six months had been until Gianna. Or how much he didn't want to be just friends with her.

He concentrated on her pleasure, touching her breasts, finding the place on her thigh that made her breath come faster, kissing a certain spot near her ear that made her moan. And he couldn't hold back any longer. He entered her and brought her to the peak where she cried out with satisfaction. A heartbeat or two behind her, his release came sooner than he would have liked.

But they had all night.

He pulled her against him and felt her hand on his chest. "You're the reason I didn't go to Los Angeles sooner."

"Me?" Her voice was a little breathless, a little sleepy.

"I couldn't leave you on Christmas." Or any other time, he added to himself.

"Merry Christmas, Shane." She snuggled into him and relaxed, quickly falling asleep in his arms.

"And to all a good night," he whispered, kissing her forehead.

The journey he'd started in June had brought him to an unexpected place and the future was still unsettled. He wasn't sure where he and Gianna went from here because Thunder Canyon wasn't big enough for him and the half brothers who wanted nothing to do with him.

Chapter Fourteen

Gianna stretched sleepily and touched something that felt a lot like a man's broad back. That didn't happen often in her world so she opened one eye and grinned from ear to ear. *Merry Christmas to me,* she thought. Memories of loving Shane the night before warmed her everywhere. He hadn't said he loved her, but he hadn't turned his back. Metaphorically speaking, since she was loving the view of his very real, very wide shoulders.

"I can feel you looking at me." Shane's voice was raspy with sleep and tinged with amusement.

"How did you know?"

"Like I said—I can feel it." He rolled over and pulled her against him, resting his chin on her hair. "Merry Christmas."

"Merry Christmas, Shane." She snuggled her cheek on his chest and caught a glimpse of his digital clock on the nightstand. "Holy cow. We have to get moving. There's a plane to catch and I bet you're not packed. All my stuff is at my apartment and I have to do an overhaul—hair, makeup, just the right outfit—before flying to Los Angeles."

"Why? You're beautiful."

"Thank you." The compliment made her glow from head to toe, but a look for meeting his folks didn't happen without some effort. "But your family will be there."

"Yeah." He laughed. "What with Christmas dinner being at their house and all."

"Right. And I can't meet them for the first time looking like I just rolled out of your bed."

"Why not?" He tipped her chin up and their gazes locked. "I like you right where you are."

"Shane—"

"Okay." He kissed the tip of her nose. "But let's have coffee. We've got time. Weather's good. I've been watching the forecast all week. Flights will be on time. We'll be having Christmas dinner in L.A."

"And I have to look fabulous."

He rolled out of bed and picked up his jeans, then slid them on. "You need to stop worrying so much."

"And you need to start worrying just a little more."

Gianna got up and grabbed his long-sleeved white shirt. She was feeling a little shy, even though last night he'd seen every inch of her naked. The soft cotton was like wrapping herself in the scent of him and came down to midthigh. She buttoned it as she followed him to the kitchen.

Resting her elbows on the granite countertop, she watched him put warm water in a state-of-the-art coffeemaker that had more bells and whistles than her car. He ground up beans then added them to the disposable filter before pushing some of those bells and whistles. Several moments later the thing started to sizzle and spit.

He turned toward her. "It won't be long now."

"Okay."

She'd have said okay to anything. The sight of his bare chest and the dusting of hair that narrowed down his belly to the vee where his jeans were unbuttoned absolutely mesmerized her. Tingles danced up and down her spine and for a second she thought there was a tune involved. Then she realized it was the doorbell.

"Are you expecting someone?"

"No. It's probably whoever is manning the front desk."

"On Christmas?"

"It's part of the job, like bringing my car to the restaurant." He shrugged. "Someone might have dropped off a package and the front desk is delivering. I'll be right back."

Gianna listened to the front door open then heard a very loud, "Surprise! Merry Christmas!"

Shane's voice drifted to her as he said, "Mom. Dad. Wow. Ryan and Maggie, too."

His family was here? *Now?* Gianna's heart started pounding as she frantically looked around for an escape route. There wasn't a cupboard big enough in the kitchen to hide her and no way to make it to the bedroom without being seen. She was pretty sure Shane didn't have an apron as he wasn't an apron-wearing sort of guy. It was just a case of being royally up doo-doo creek. This was like the bad dream where you somehow ended up in the mall ladies' room naked to the waist with no choice except to suck it up and walk out, knowing humiliation would happen no matter how much you pretended otherwise.

It would just be worse the longer she stayed put so, head held high, she moved just into the kitchen doorway, visible from the living room where the Roarke family stood. It was clear they all saw her because suddenly everyone went silent.

"Merry Christmas," she said, forcing cheerfulness into her voice.

"You must be Gianna Garrison." An attractive older woman with a stylish brunette bob separated from the group. "Shane said you were a blue-eyed redhead."

She touched a tousled curl by her cheek. "Guilty."

The woman, who had to be his mother, laughed. "He said you were friends."

Shane moved beside her, his expression sheepish and apologetic. "It was an ambush phone call, I was under oath and she was cross-examining me."

"He gets that a lot." The older man, obviously his father, had silver hair, very distinguished-looking. "I'm Gavin Roarke."

"My dad," Shane confirmed. "This is my mom, Christa. That's my little brother, Ryan and baby sister, Maggie."

"Hi." Gianna smiled as confidently as possible at the tall, good-looking guy with brown hair and eyes. His sister was wearing a navy knit hat pulled over long blond hair that spilled down her back.

"Are you surprised?" Maggie asked.

"Yes. Now, what are you guys doing here?"

"Your mother wanted to be with you for Christmas," Gavin explained.

"What part of me flying out for dinner did you not understand?"

"It's a mom thing." Christa's shrug was apologetic. "I miss the days when you guys were kids and ripped into presents first thing. You're all grown up so the best we could do is surprise you and be here in the morning."

"So you took a red eye?" Shane asked, shock and pleasure mixing in his voice.

"Yes," Gavin said. "Your brother and sister haven't stopped whining about it yet."

"But I'd do it all again just to see the look on your face. And everything," Ryan said, sliding a glance at Gianna's bare legs and feet, then grinning at his older brother's obvious discomfort. There was no way his family didn't know they'd slept together.

"I can't believe we actually pulled off this surprise," Maggie said. "It's nice to meet you, Gianna."

"Likewise." She was trying to hide behind Shane. "I usually look so much better than this."

"You look fine," Christa said and sounded like she meant it sincerely. "Attractive doesn't do her justice, Shane."

"Attractive was the best you could do?" Gianna didn't know whether to be flattered or not.

Looking down, Shane met her gaze. "Again, under oath."

"Don't pay any attention to him," his mother scoffed. "You're stunning. And all my children will tell you that I don't say anything I don't mean."

"It's true. She doesn't suck up," Ryan agreed. "So, about last night—"

"There's coffee in the kitchen." Shane cocked his thumb toward the room behind them. "I'm going to put on a shirt."

"Preferably not this one." As they laughed, Gianna sidled in the direction of the master bedroom and after going into the hallway, she turned and ran.

She grabbed her things from the floor where Shane had tossed her sweater and jeans last night. It seemed the arms and legs were pulled inside out. That happened when someone was in a big hurry to get your clothes off. Quickly she put them back on while Shane dressed.

"I can't believe this is happening. I just said I didn't want to meet your family looking like I rolled out of your bed. It's official. I'm being punished because I did just roll out of your bed." She turned a pleading look on him. "Tell me there's a back way out."

"Sorry." He moved in front of her and cupped her face in his palms. "They love you."

"We barely met. And I do mean barely what with wearing nothing but your shirt. There's no way they like me."

"They do. I know them and there was nothing but approval. Now let's have coffee."

When they returned, only his parents were there. Shane glanced at them, surprised. "So much for being together this morning. Ryan couldn't wait ten minutes to start checking out Thunder Canyon women."

"He does have a talent for that," his mother said, fondness and exasperation swirling in her eyes. "Although I do wish he'd find the right one and settle down. But, no. He and Maggie are using your guest rooms for a cat nap. They've been up all night."

"So have you guys," Shane pointed out.

"And worth it. But those two…" Christa shook her head sympathetically. "Rookies. It doesn't matter that you're all grown up, your father and I remember being up all night with babies. We've still got it, don't we, Gavin?"

He put his arm around her shoulders. "We do, indeed."

His mother's eyes were suspiciously bright. "'Tis the season to be with the ones you love."

"Yes, it is." Shane walked over and kissed her cheek. "Can I buy you a cup of coffee?"

"Sounds heavenly."

When they were settled around the table in the kitchen, his mother said, "So, you seem much more relaxed than you did last time we talked."

"Yeah." Shane picked up his steaming mug. "I found my biological mother and father."

Gavin exchanged a glance with his wife before asking, "Do you want to talk about it?"

"Of course. You're my parents." He took a deep breath

and said, "Grace Smith died a long time ago, when her sons were pretty young."

"You have brothers." It wasn't a question and Christa's tone was carefully neutral.

"Yes. But they're not happy about it. My birth father's name is Arthur Swinton and he did some bad things, to them and the town. He's in prison."

"Oh, my—" Christa shook her head. "You tease me about having a gift for words, but at this moment I'm at a complete loss."

"It's really complicated," Gianna said. "Grace was pregnant with Shane and didn't tell Arthur. He was so in love with her and couldn't accept that she loved another man. It made him a little crazy."

The other woman studied her son. "How do you feel about all that?"

"I had a rough time in the beginning," he admitted. "I've come to love this town and finding out you're the son of public enemy number one was hard." He set his coffee down and took Gianna's hand. "But I got lucky. My *friend* talked me through it."

"I'm glad Shane has you," his mother said.

"Me, too. No one should have to go through something like that alone."

Shane squeezed her fingers. "I've been thinking, Mom. Since there are four lawyers in the family, maybe something can be done for Arthur."

That surprised Gianna. He hadn't said anything to her, but she approved. The man wasn't a danger to society. His was a crime of revenge and it was over now.

"We can look into his case," Gavin said. "There might be mitigating circumstances to bring before a judge when he's up for parole. If he can return the money he took while on the city council there could be a reduced sentence. Time off for good behavior."

"Thanks. You guys are—" Shane's voice caught. "I got really lucky when you picked me."

"We're the lucky ones," his mother said. "We loved you the moment we laid eyes on you, so tiny and sweet. Instantly I felt as if you were meant for us. All I ever wanted was for you to be happy. I hope that everything you found out will help you to find serenity and stop searching. Stop running."

"I have." He met Gianna's gaze, but his own was impossible to read.

She had no idea what he meant, but if she'd helped him find peace, that would have to be good enough.

"That was the best Christmas dinner ever." Maggie Roarke leaned back in her chair and groaned dramatically. "I've never been so full in my life."

Gianna glanced around Shane's dining-room table, set for six. He sat at one end, she at the other, sort of host and hostess. His parents, Maggie and Ryan were on either side, facing each other. The big windows made the majestic, snow-covered mountains an extension of the room and gave them a spectacular view.

"I'm glad you liked the food, little sister." Shane sipped his chardonnay. "When you drop in on a guy, you take potluck."

"Then we should drop in every weekend," his mother said. "That beef Wellington is, without a doubt, the best thing I've ever had."

He'd never looked so pleased and personally satisfied at work. "If I hadn't been able to pillage stuff from the restaurant it would have been grilled cheese."

"Right," his brother scoffed. "So speaks the cooking genius who won *If You Can't Stand the Heat* by putting together a little something with lima beans, honey and tofu."

"You're exaggerating."

"Maybe just a little," Ryan admitted. "I don't think even you could make something edible out of that."

"Never underestimate the palate appeal of tofu," Shane said.

Gianna loved watching him banter with his family and was very happy to be included in the group. She'd been looking forward to the trip to L.A., but didn't mind that the plans were altered. This was one of the best holidays ever. Her financial position hadn't changed, but she was rich in so many other ways.

Definitely there'd been recent ups and downs, but today had been perfect, if you didn't count meeting the Roarkes wearing nothing but Shane's shirt. While his family napped, he'd driven her home to clean up, then they'd stopped by The Gallatin Room to get what he needed for dinner. Judging by the satisfied groans all around, he was a smashing success.

His mother looked out the window and sighed. "I can see why your voice was full of reverence when you told me about Thunder Canyon. It certainly is beautiful. God's country."

"Amen," her husband said.

Gianna couldn't agree more. She'd come home with her tail between her legs, feeling like a failure, but somehow this place had healed her soul. Her heart was in jeopardy, but maybe life was always a trade-off.

"It makes you hardly notice that your place has no Christmas decorations," Maggie said. "Next year."

"Maybe." Shane's tone was noncommittal.

"I'm going to earn my keep and clear the table." Gianna stood and started stacking plates.

"I'll help you."

When his mother started to stand, Shane stopped her. "No, you don't."

"I'm not a guest," she protested.

"Tomorrow you can help. But you were up all night getting here. That buys you a pass on doing dishes. All of you," he said, looking at each of them in turn.

"He just wants to be alone with Gianna," Ryan teased. "If you can't stand the heat…"

Shane lifted one eyebrow at his brother. "Can you blame me?"

"No."

Gianna blushed. Ryan grinned. Shane glared.

While Shane stacked plates at the other end of the table, she carried hers to the kitchen. Behind her she heard his mother say, "You two make a good team."

Gianna thought so, but what did she know. Her judgment was questionable. She was the one who'd wasted so much time on the wrong guys. After setting dishes in the sink, she turned to go back for the rest, but Shane was right behind her.

"I'll get the food," he said, turning back the way he'd come.

That was her prompt to rinse and arrange the plates and silverware in the dishwasher. By the time she'd finished, he was putting leftovers in the refrigerator, beside the pumpkin chiffon pie he'd "borrowed" from the restaurant freezer, from the stock he'd made for the restaurant's holiday menu.

"Do you want to wait to serve dessert?" she asked.

"Good idea."

They assembled small plates and forks. He got coffee ready but didn't push the "on" button. Then they looked at each other.

"Christmas is almost over," he said.

"I know. At the same time I'm relieved, it kind of makes me sad."

"Did you get everything you wanted?"

"I love the perfume," she said, not really answering.

His question made her think and not about the gift he'd given her. There was only one thing that could possibly make this day perfect and it couldn't be bought in a store. She just wanted to hear that he cared.

"How about you?" she countered. "Did you get everything?"

"Almost." He rubbed the back of his neck. "It's silly, I guess. And unrealistic given the circumstances. But I'd hoped to talk to D.J. and Dax. It's not that I'm looking to be embraced as a brother. I'm not asking for a kidney or bone marrow transplant."

"But?"

"I like them." He shrugged. "It was natural. I'm going to miss the friendship."

"That could still happen. Your paths are bound to cross if you stay in Thunder Canyon." She still didn't know what his long-term plans were.

"What about you?" The question turned the conversation away from him, his goals. "Is traveling still what you want?"

What she wanted had certainly changed since she'd returned to her hometown. She'd thought she was confused and lost then, but the feeling had multiplied a hundred fold. There was only one point she was clear on.

Gianna looked up at him. "In the last six months I've found out that Thunder Canyon is in my blood. I was so anxious to get away, but now I can't imagine being gone forever. I saw this place through your eyes and fell in love with it all over again." She left out the part about falling in love with him at the same time.

"I know what you mean."

"So, I'm going to put my business degree to work as soon as I figure out what business *will* work."

He nodded and a dark expression settled on his face. "There's something I have to say."

Gianna didn't like the sound of that. It was the male version of "we have to talk" and it was never about anything good. But she'd wasted a lot of time on relationships that didn't work. If this "thing" with them was heading over a cliff, it would be best to find out now. Knowing wouldn't stop the hurt, but… She couldn't really think of an upside to knowing. Best get it over with.

"Okay. What's on your mind?"

"You and I," he started. "And the Traubs. There are a lot of them here in town. Based on D.J.'s reaction, when he tells the rest of the family about who I am. They're not going to like me much either. You know I care about you, but—"

She held up her hand. "Don't say it. I hate that word."

"Gianna—" He shook his head. "You want to make a life here. If you get hooked up with me that could get awkward and I'd do anything to keep you from being hurt."

"Really? You're actually saying that this town isn't big enough for both of you?"

"I know it sounds like something from a bad Western, but yeah, I am. And there's only one way to keep you out of it."

"You don't have to protect me."

"I can't help it where you're concerned."

He was talking about walking away. He was willing to give up a place that had touched his soul. But this wasn't a decision that just affected him and she should get a say in it.

"Look," she said, "It's not—"

"Shane?" His father was standing in the doorway and neither of them had noticed.

"Yeah, Dad?"

"There's someone at your front door. A young man. He says he'd like to speak with you."

Shane straightened away from the counter looking as surprised as she felt. "That's odd. I wasn't expecting anyone. Did he say what it's about or give you his name?"

Gavin shook his head. "He only said that he needed a few minutes of your time."

"Okay. I'll see what he wants."

Gianna had a bad feeling. This was like getting a phone call in the middle of the night. Someone stopping by unannounced this late on Christmas just felt weird. And that's why she walked to the door with Shane. He wasn't the only one who couldn't help going into protective mode. When she saw who was standing there, she slipped her hand into his.

"Hello, Dax. Merry Christmas."

"Shane. Same to you." If Dax Traub was surprised at the two of them together, he didn't show it.

"What can I do for you?"

"I have a favor to ask."

"What?" Shane's voice was neutral, but the rest of him tensed.

"I'd like to talk to you."

"My family is in from L.A."

"Sorry to interrupt your Christmas." Dax glanced into the room behind them. "Here isn't what I had in mind, anyway. Can you meet me at the Rib Shack? It won't take long."

The bad stuff didn't usually take very long to say. Shane's peace-on-earth expression disappeared, replaced by the intensity he'd worn like armor for the past six months. And Gianna couldn't blame him.

The two men stared at each other for several moments while Shane thought it over. Finally he said, "I'll meet you there. Is now okay?"

Dax nodded. "Thanks, Shane."

Gianna watched him walk down the hall to the elevator and her bad feeling got bigger. "Don't go, Shane. Whatever he has to say can wait until tomorrow when it's not Christmas."

"I want to get this over with. The sooner, the better."

Never would be better as far as Gianna was concerned.

Chapter Fifteen

On the short drive to the Rib Shack, Shane kept picturing Gianna's face, the stubborn tilt of her chin, the way her full mouth pulled tight with anger. He couldn't help thinking she was beautiful when she was angry. First, she'd been revving up to talk him out of leaving town, when he'd told her that things would be awkward with the Traubs.

They'd lived in Thunder Canyon for a long time. He was the newcomer who'd had ulterior motives and was the son of their enemy. It was a stigma that would stick; it would rub off on Gianna and her family. She'd found her way back and knew what she wanted. He wouldn't jeopardize that for her, which was why he had to do the right thing and go quietly.

He loved her too much to ruin her life by being in it.

Second, he'd had to talk her out of coming with him for this conversation with Dax. She would take his side against the Traubs. It's just the way she was and he couldn't let her do it. What finally convinced her to stay put was when he asked her to watch over his family. With her they were in good hands. And now it was time for the showdown.

The Rib Shack parking lot had a few cars, but it looked pretty quiet this late on Christmas. Holiday hours were posted inside for the guests staying at the resort, but he knew the restaurant was closed to the public now. He parked by the outside entrance; it would make for a quick exit.

"Best get this over with," he muttered.

"This" being the portion of the holiday entertainment where he was run out of town. He was stubborn enough to tell them to shove it, but for Gianna's sake he would listen politely then walk away. He wouldn't ask her to choose between the town and family she loved.

But, he'd learned something from his biological mother. Grace Smith Traub had shown him that the greatest love of all is letting someone go to give them a better life.

He walked through the parking lot as snowflakes started to fall and his breath made clouds in front of his face. As he opened the door and went inside the restaurant, the sounds of talking, laughter and children playing drifted to him. It pierced the loneliness that pressed heavily on his heart.

In the Rib Shack's main dining room, tables were pushed together to accommodate a large group—all of them Traubs as far as he could tell. He recognized Jason, who'd come from Texas to settle here. Clay, Antonia and their little ones were next to him. Forrest Traub and Angie Anderson sat so close together you couldn't see space between them. There were a couple more guys he didn't recognize, but they were Traubs, what with that strong family-resemblance thing.

As he moved farther into the room, conversation around the table stopped and everyone looked at him. When Dax angled his head, D.J. and Clay stood up, as if it was a strategy agreed on ahead of time. The three of them moved to meet him.

Dax slid his fingertips into the pockets of his jeans. "Thanks for coming, Shane."

"No problem. Looks like the gang's all here," he said.

"Not everyone could make it." Clay glanced over his shoulder at the group. "But there were too many to fit in anyone's house. D.J. volunteered the Shack for Christmas dinner."

Shane looked at the man in question who still hadn't said anything. The last time he'd been here, D.J. had thrown him out.

"We've got some things to say. Let's sit over there where it's quiet," Dax suggested, pointing to a far corner. "Otherwise the kids will drive you crazy."

That was a kind of crazy Shane wanted, but had given up hope he would ever have. Without a word, he followed the other men to the table all by itself in the big room. He had a feeling this wasn't so much about quiet as it was about protecting the women and children from the ugliness of the past, the flaw in him that was all about who his father was.

After the four of them took seats around the table, Dax looked at his cousin Clay, a look that said "get ready." "Some information has come to our attention."

Shane knew Clay was from Rust Creek where another branch of the family lived. He had the same Traub features—tall, muscular, dark hair and brown eyes. He was a little younger than the other two men and more boyish-looking. Although not now with intensity darkening his eyes and tension in his face.

Dax nodded at him. "Tell Shane what you told us."

"When I was a little kid…" Clay blew out a breath, then continued. "I overheard my parents arguing about Aunt Grace and Uncle Doug, Dax and D.J.'s parents. My mom just didn't understand how Grace could give away her own child then act as if he'd never existed. She was angry that

Uncle Doug didn't support her through it. Dad said that his brother would have had a hard time raising a child that wasn't his, but that ticked Mom off even more. She said Doug should have been man enough to put that aside for the sake of the baby, the child of the woman he loved." He shrugged at his cousins. "I only remembered recently. But when I was clear about the memory, I knew Dax and D.J. had a brother out there somewhere."

"Me." Shane looked at each man.

Dax nodded. "Clay wasn't sure whether or not to say anything to D.J. and me. Obviously that wasn't our father's finest hour."

"Or our mother's," D.J. added.

His brother nodded darkly. "We had a get-together last night for Christmas Eve and were talking about why the two sides of the family have been estranged all these years. Clay told us what he remembered. Then D.J. mentioned the conversation with you."

Shane looked at the man who looked so much like him. "The one where I told him about your mother and Arthur Swinton having an affair."

He waited for the explosion, but the two men didn't say a word. They looked shell-shocked and he realized the revelations were too recent. They needed time to take it all in.

"Look, I didn't come to Thunder Canyon to make trouble, just to find my birth parents. I did that. I'm sorry it involves your mother. I get that you don't want to believe it. But that doesn't change—"

Clay held up a hand. "D.J. told us what he said to you, but if you could cut him some slack... Just put yourself in his place. He had no reason to believe you. His mom died when he was a kid and his dad wasn't likely to bring up the subject." He rubbed a hand across the back of his neck. "But my parents knew Grace Smith had a baby and gave him up for adoption. They confirmed everything and it's why the two families had a falling out all those years ago."

"I didn't know any of this," D.J. confirmed. "Then you tell me my mother had a thing with Arthur Swinton. I thought you were lying and I couldn't figure out why you'd do that."

Shane figured he'd have felt the same if someone came to him with a wild story like this. All he could do now was reassure them. "I'm not looking for anything but the facts. If you want, we can do DNA tests to prove the truth once and for all."

"No." D.J. shook his head. "As soon as I calmed down, I realized all the evidence was right in front of me. Our personalities clicked. Similar sense of humor. I felt an almost instant connection."

"Then there was the strong resemblance that Allaire saw," Dax said.

His brother nodded. "We bonded right away, without even knowing the family link. It struck a chord that felt true. Then Clay tied everything together with what he remembered and we talked to Uncle Bob and Aunt Ellie, who confirmed his memory and everything else. We don't have any doubts."

Maybe not about being brothers, Shane realized. But there was still the fact of his father. He met their gazes, but this had to be said. "I know how you feel about Arthur Swinton."

The statement hung in the air and he knew they were filling in the blanks. His father was a criminal. But Gianna was right about him. "There's no reason you should believe this, but Arthur isn't a bad man. He loved our mother. Still does."

"You saw him in jail?" D.J. looked surprised.

"Yeah. He didn't know about me. She never said anything about being pregnant. No one should be too hard on her. Think about it. She was just a teenager. Scared. Under pressure from her family. I'm not judging and you shouldn't, either. No one's perfect and she was just doing what she thought was right for her family."

"I hear you," Dax said. "But it will take some time to work this through."

Shane nodded. "And I'm not saying Arthur deserves forgiveness, but he's a broken man. When she turned her back on him, he went off the deep end. He only saw that you all had her and he was left out in the cold."

"I'm not sure I can ever forgive him. He put me, my family and this town through a lot," D.J. said quietly.

Shane nodded. "I'd never tell you what to do, it's just that—"

"You're not like him," D.J. finished. "He couldn't handle what life threw at him, but it's not in the DNA."

"Pretty much." Shane was grateful he didn't have to make the case, that they got it. "I couldn't have said it better."

"It's a brother thing, I guess." D.J. stood and held out his hand. "I'm sorry for what I said."

"You mean the part where you threw me out of here?" Shane teased.

"That, too. I realized that in your shoes I'd have come looking for who I was. I'm sorry I was so hard on you."

"Forget it." Shane stood and took the other man's hand.

"Welcome to the family." D.J. pulled him into a quick bro hug.

Then it was Dax's turn. "Better late than never."

"Can't argue with that."

Shane remembered his dismissive comment to Gianna that you couldn't have too much family and knew now he was right about that. "This is a pretty good Christmas present."

"You're not getting mushy, are you?" D.J. joked.

"Of course not. You couldn't handle it."

And just like that they slipped into the teasing, macho banter thing that brothers did. It finally felt as if the last loose piece inside him clicked into place.

"Come on over and join the family," Dax said, indicating the gathering on the other side of the room.

"Can I get a rain check?" Shane asked. "Gianna is waiting for me—"

"I knew it," D.J. said. "There's something between you two, isn't there?"

"You're not matchmaking, are you?" Shane answered without answering.

"I don't have to. It's too late for that."

Shane just grinned at his brothers. The only thing that could keep him from joining the family group was Gianna. She'd been with him almost every step of the way. Even tonight she hadn't wanted him to be alone meeting his brothers and he wouldn't leave her alone any longer.

He had some things to say to her.

When she wasn't pacing, Gianna stood in front of the tall windows in Shane's living room, staring outside. It was a serene view most of the time, but not now. His family was watching a Christmas movie in the media room and had asked her to join them, but she couldn't sit still.

She shouldn't have let him go alone. D.J. was her friend. Maybe she could have been a bridge, helped the Traubs understand why he'd quietly gathered information instead of walking into their lives with guns blazing.

"Gianna?"

She turned and saw his mother. "Mrs. Roarke—"

"Please call me Christa. We're going to be seeing a lot of each other." There was a twinkle in her eyes.

Just a guess, but it seemed as if his mother was thinking there was something serious going on between her and Shane. It was serious, all right, but not in a good way. After learning that love had destroyed his father, it wasn't likely Shane would give it a try.

If Dax hadn't interrupted them, he would have told her he was leaving and they were over before even really getting started. Any second she expected Shane would come back and do just that. It was about protecting himself as well as her, but that didn't take the hurt away.

"Please tell me what's going on," Christa said.

"I'm not sure what you mean." That was lame and Gianna knew it. The woman was an attorney, for God's sake. Like she couldn't tell when someone was stalling?

"All right. I'll put a finer point on it. A man comes to see my son and he leaves. Now you're about to wear a hole in the floor from pacing." The woman's eyes narrowed on her. "Is he in some kind of trouble?"

"No." Probably not. She didn't think any punches were being thrown. All of them were too civilized for that, right? Except the information Shane had uncovered challenged all the Traubs' beliefs about their mother.

"Then why did he leave?" Christa asked.

Gianna didn't know what to do. This was Shane's journey, his story to tell, and should be done his way.

"He just went to the Rib Shack. It's a restaurant at Thunder Canyon Resort where they serve—ribs." She was babbling. And stalling.

"Imagine that." The woman gave her a "mom look," the expression specially designed to intimidate anyone under the age of forty.

"They're really good ribs," she said, all confidence leaking out of her voice. "A special sauce. Secret recipe."

"Uh-huh." Christa moved closer and there was understanding in her eyes. "Look, sweetheart, it's clear that you're trying to protect him and as his mother, I'm all for that. But if he needs help we need to go to him—"

At that moment the front door opened and closed, and Shane walked into the room. "Hi."

"You're back." Duh.

Gianna studied him and thank goodness he looked all right. No bruises or blood, but his expression gave no clue about what had happened.

"Shane, what's going on?" Christa asked. "Why did you disappear with that man?"

"Don't worry, Mom. Everything's fine. I'll tell you all about it later."

His mother studied him for several moments and seemed to see what she needed to. "You look all right. I'd know if you weren't. When you're ready to talk I'll be watching that hilarious Christmas movie about the little boy and the gun."

"Okay, Mom." When she started to walk away he said, "I love you."

She smiled. "I love you, too, son."

When she was gone, Shane said to Gianna, "We need to talk. Privately."

"Okay, but first—"

Without another word he took her arm and steered her to the French door. After opening it, he linked his fingers with hers, then led her outside.

"It's snowing," she said, blinking away the flakes that drifted into her eyes when she looked up at the sky.

"A white Christmas. That makes this an almost perfect day." He took off his jacket and dragged it around her shoulders. "There's just one more thing."

Perfect day? Not from her perspective. "What happened with Dax and D.J.?"

"I found my brothers," he said simply.

"That's not a news flash. What did they say?"

"That they're my brothers. If Ryan were here he'd say, 'What am I? Chopped liver?' The thing is, I love him, my whole family. I'd do anything for them."

"They feel the same about you." His mother had been this close to going to the Rib Shack to do battle with whoever might be hurting him.

"That's what makes it so hard to explain why getting to know the brothers who share my blood was so important." He dragged his hand through his hair. "I feel as if I've found the missing part of myself. But that implies that Mom, Dad, Ryan and Maggie aren't enough. And that's just not true."

"I think they understand. After all, your mother started this search. She knew you needed to find yourself."

"And I did."

"So, I guess Dax and D.J. had a change of heart and believed you?"

"Yeah. They're still reeling from the whole thing, but they welcomed me to the family."

"That means the Traubs and the Roarkes are all related, too."

"One big happy family. No one shut out," he said thoughtfully. "Like Arthur."

"I know. Thinking about that makes me sad for him."

"That's his cross to bear, but I can't hate him for it. My mother was a good woman, only trying to do the right thing for everyone. I believe that she loved me and wanted me in a place where I'd have a fresh start, no black mark to start life with. As for Arthur..." He was thoughtful for a moment. "He just loved too deeply a woman he could never have." He held the sides of his jacket together under her chin. "Now that I finally know who I am, I understand things about myself."

"Like what?"

"I've been running from life, but no more. When I

couldn't get on that plane it had nothing to do with the restaurant or a holiday plan. It was because of you. Through every important step on this journey of self-discovery I wasn't alone because you wouldn't let me be."

"It just wasn't right."

"Leaving you meant choosing to be alone and I couldn't do it."

He smiled down at her, then put his arm around her shoulders and held her close. Side by side they stared at the lights on the ski lift in the mountains.

"It was right here that I fell in love with Thunder Canyon." He met her gaze. "And right here where I fell in love with you."

She hadn't dared to hope and wasn't quite sure she'd heard right. "You fell in love with me? Right here?"

"Yes."

"But you didn't even kiss me that night," she reminded him.

"I was running then. How could I commit or ask you to when I didn't understand who I was? Now I know I'm a man who feels passionately, like my father. Except my story will have a happy ending because I don't intend to let you get away."

She rested her cheek on his chest, feeling the strong, steady beat of his heart, a rhythm that matched her own. "I assume you have a plan?"

"I do. First I want you to marry me."

She lifted her head and stared up at him. "I thought you were leaving Thunder Canyon."

"I want to put down roots here. Make this home base. I want you to be my partner in business and in life. With your experience and support, I believe together we can build a ridiculously successful restaurant empire and an even better marriage."

"Oh, Shane, I can't believe it—" Emotion choked off her words for a moment. "I didn't think it was possible to be so happy."

"I've never wanted anything as passionately as I want you, to have a family with you." He took her hands into his. "If I wasn't so dense I'd have bought you a ring, but we'll fix that as soon as the jewelry store opens tomorrow. Right now I just want you to say yes. I need to hear you say it because loving you is food to my soul."

"Yes. Yes. Yes. I love you so much." She threw her arms around his neck. "This is the best Christmas present ever. And you're right. This makes it an absolutely perfect day. Because 'tis the season of love."

He held her as if he'd never let her go. "That means every day for the rest of our lives will be like Christmas."

"And no mistletoe required. All I need is you."

* * * * *

Turn the page for a preview of
THE OTHER SIDE OF US
by
Sarah Mayberry,

coming January 2013
from Harlequin® Superromance®.

PLUS, exciting changes are in the works!
Enjoy the same great stories in a longer format
and new look—beginning January 2013!

Coming January 2013

THE OTHER SIDE OF US
A brand-new novel
from Harlequin® Superromance® author
Sarah Mayberry

*In recovery from a serious accident, Mackenzie Williams
is beating all the doctors' predictions. But she needs
single-minded focus. She* doesn't *need the distraction
of neighbors—especially good-looking ones
like Oliver Garrett!*

MACKENZIE BREATHED DEEPLY to recover from the work-out. She'd pushed herself too far but she wanted to accelerate her rehabilitation. Still, she needed to lie down to combat the nausea and shaking muscles.

There was a knock on the front door. Who on earth would be visiting her on a Thursday morning? Probably a cold-calling salesperson.

She answered, but her pithy rejection died before she'd formed the first words.

The man on her doorstep was definitely not a cold caller. Nothing about this man was cold, from the auburn of his wavy hair to his brown eyes to his sensual mouth. Nothing cold about those broad shoulders, flat belly and lean hips, either.

"Hey," he said in a shiver-inducing baritone. "I'm Oliver Garrett. I moved in next door." His smile was so warm and vibrant it was almost offensive.

"Mackenzie Williams." Oh, no. Her legs were starting to

HSREXP1212HH

tremble, indicating they wouldn't hold up long. Any second now she would embarrass herself in front of this complete and very good-looking stranger.

"It's been years since I was down here." He seemed to settle in for a chat. "It doesn't look as though—"

"I have to go." Her stomach rolled as she shut the door. The last thing she registered was the look of shock on Oliver's face at her abrupt dismissal.

And somehow she knew their neighborly relations would be a lot cooler now.

Will Mackenzie be able to make it up to Oliver for her rude introduction?
Find out in THE OTHER SIDE OF US
by Sarah Mayberry, available January 2013 from Harlequin® Superromance®. PLUS, exciting changes are in the works! Enjoy the same great stories in a longer format and new look—beginning January 2013!

HSREXP1212HH

REQUEST YOUR FREE BOOKS!

2 FREE NOVELS PLUS 2 FREE GIFTS!

◆ Harlequin®

SPECIAL EDITION

Life, Love & Family

YES! Please send me 2 FREE Harlequin® Special Edition novels and my 2 FREE gifts (gifts are worth about $10). After receiving them, if I don't wish to receive any more books, I can return the shipping statement marked "cancel." If I don't cancel, I will receive 6 brand-new novels every month and be billed just $4.49 per book in the U.S. or $5.24 per book in Canada. That's a saving of at least 14% off the cover price! It's quite a bargain! Shipping and handling is just 50¢ per book in the U.S. and 75¢ per book in Canada.* I understand that accepting the 2 free books and gifts places me under no obligation to buy anything. I can always return a shipment and cancel at any time. Even if I never buy another book, the two free books and gifts are mine to keep forever.

235/335 HDN FEGF

Name _____ (PLEASE PRINT)

Address _____ Apt. #

City _____ State/Prov. _____ Zip/Postal Code

Signature (if under 18, a parent or guardian must sign)

Mail to the Reader Service:
IN U.S.A.: P.O. Box 1867, Buffalo, NY 14240-1867
IN CANADA: P.O. Box 609, Fort Erie, Ontario L2A 5X3

Not valid for current subscribers to Harlequin Special Edition books.

Want to try two free books from another line?
Call 1-800-873-8635 or visit www.ReaderService.com.

* Terms and prices subject to change without notice. Prices do not include applicable taxes. Sales tax applicable in N.Y. Canadian residents will be charged applicable taxes. Offer not valid in Quebec. This offer is limited to one order per household. All orders subject to credit approval. Credit or debit balances in a customer's account(s) may be offset by any other outstanding balance owed by or to the customer. Please allow 4 to 6 weeks for delivery. Offer available while quantities last.

Your Privacy—The Reader Service is committed to protecting your privacy. Our Privacy Policy is available online at www.ReaderService.com or upon request from the Reader Service.

We make a portion of our mailing list available to reputable third parties that offer products we believe may interest you. If you prefer that we not exchange your name with third parties, or if you wish to clarify or modify your communication preferences, please visit us at www.ReaderService.com/consumerschoice or write to us at Reader Service Preference Service, P.O. Box 9062, Buffalo, NY 14269. Include your complete name and address.

HSE11B

It all starts with a kiss

Check out the brand-new series

HARLEQUIN® KISS™

Fun, flirty and sensual romances.
ON SALE JANUARY 22!

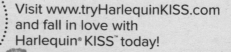